THE Swan MAIDEN

THE Swan MAIDEN

Serene Conneeley

Blessed Bee Books

The freedom to be your true self is just
as important, just as essential to life,
as loving and being loved...

THE SWAN MAIDEN
An Australian Faery Tale

First edition copyright © Serene Conneeley 2020

Conneeley, Serene
The Swan Maiden by Serene Conneeley
ISBN: 978-0-6484016-3-6

Website: www.SereneConneeley.com
Email: serene@sereneconneeley.com

Published by Blessed Bee Books
PO Box 449, Newtown, NSW 2042
Australia

Front cover © KILA Designs, www.kiladesigns.com.au
Interiors: Serene Conneeley
Swan Maiden photo: Jessica Truscott @faestock
Black swan photo: Peter Hermes Furian
Swan illustrations: Lorelyn Medina and Christine Krahl

"Yes, your transformation will be hard.
Yes, you'll feel frightened, messed up and knocked down.
Yes, you'll want to stop.
Yes, it's the best work you'll ever do."
Robin Sharma, Canadian writer

Chapter 1

"Mummy, Mummy, come quick! Look at the swans!" The little girl in the sparkly purple t-shirt and green shorts ran across the grass, her gait awkward, but she only giggled when she swayed to the left, quickly rebalancing herself and continuing down the slope.

The woman laughed gaily and chased after her daughter. She didn't bother telling her to be careful, like so many other parents, because she knew that life had to be lived for every moment, and learning to get back up again was a far more precious lesson than never having the chance to fall in the first place.

The black swan gliding so elegantly across the lake had seen the child trip and fall a few times in her eagerness to get down to the water. It had shocked the little girl the

first time it happened – she'd sat up in a daze and opened her mouth to wail, but her mother had just grinned and clapped her hands. "That was an excellent tumble Gracie, well done! And I'm sure you entertained all the ducks."

The little girl's lip trembled, and tears welled in her eyes, then she stared at the lake, wide-eyed with wonder, as seven ducks sailed towards her in perfect formation. Instantly forgetting the scrape on her leg and the graze on her palms, a laugh bubbled up and out of her, echoing across the surface of the water. She clapped her pudgy hands in imitation of her mother, then got to her feet and staggered closer to the shore.

Smiling, her mum took her hand and offered her some peas, and Gracie's face lit up with delight as she threw the little green balls to the approaching ducks, clapping again when one of them dove down under the surface of the lake, wiggling its bottom in the air before its head popped up again, the pea in its beak.

As she grew older, the girl came to the park just as often with her father. One day they exuberantly flew a kite together, before making their way down to the water to chat to the feathered creatures. Gracie had names for every one of them – it was she who had christened Signet and her swan family – and was always very careful to make sure every bird on the lake got something to eat. And when one of them seemed to be snatching up more than their fair share, she was hilariously fierce.

"No Sammy Swampie, that's not for you! Don't be mean to your brothers. You've had yours."

Perplexed, she turned to her father, who quickly tried to smother his laugh. "Daddy, how come they're so kind some days, and all the swamp hens take food to the little ones, but now they're being greedy gutses and refusing to share?"

Signet didn't hear the answer, distracted by a young boy who was throwing rocks at the ducks. Drawing her neck up to its full length and fluffing her feathers out to look larger than she was, she swooped across the surface of the lake, right at the boy, satisfaction washing over her as he shrieked and screamed for his parents.

"Wah! That swan is trying to attack me, but I didn't do anything!" he shouted indignantly.

"Don't worry son, we'll make the ranger get rid of it," a sweaty, red-faced man said smugly, cruelty etched in every line of his face.

Gracie put her hands on her hips, striking a defiant pose that made Signet shake with amusement. "No! You leave the beautiful swan alone. That boy was throwing rocks at the ducks. He's a meanie, and a bully. The ranger should get rid of *him*!"

Shock crossed the father's face, and he took a menacing step towards Gracie, arm raised to slap her. Then he saw the ring of concerned parents circling him, cutting him off from the girl, so he shrugged and picked up his last remaining beer.

"It's a stupid swan anyway, not worth the trouble. Let's go Tommy!" And the father and son, still grumbling under their breath, shoulders stiff with hostility, slunk away.

Gracie's father hugged her. "I'm so proud of you darling. That was a brave thing you did, standing up to the bully and protecting those who are vulnerable. And look, the swans are coming over to say thank you."

He was right. Signet and her beloved were sailing across the water to the little girl, and she squealed with delight.

Her giggles got louder when the two swans nudged their beaks at her, letting her pat their long, soft, feathery necks.

Her hand was gentle, and she spoke to them both in a low, calming murmur.

"I love you, pretty swans. And I'm sorry about the mean boy. Not all people are like that – most of us care about animals and plants and stuff. That's why Daddy and I are planting trees here later today, to make the park nicer for you too."

Then she turned her gaze to the male swan, and smiled again. "Hello Cobie. I'm so glad you two are still together. We learnt at kindergarten that swans fall in love and have the same husband or wife for life, like my mummy and daddy. That's so romantic."

Signet glowed. It really was.

The swan especially loved watching Gracie visit the park with both her parents, and she was always happy when they came as a family, pulling out a blanket and setting up their picnic down by the lake. Gracie would skip down to the shore and call out a greeting to all the water birds who flocked around her, then excitedly distribute the peas, corn and grapes she always brought with her.

The little girl was so full of joy and curiosity, and all the water creatures trusted her because of her kindness and gentle spirit. There was a light inside her that shone brightly, reflecting her hope and grace. She had been named well.

And the devotion of the child's parents, to their daughter and to each other, reminded Signet of her own partner. She'd met Cobie years ago, right here in this park, and they'd been together ever since.

Chapter 2

Feeling content, Signet pushed more reeds and twigs onto their nest, relieved that it was still mostly intact. This summer, bushfire smoke had hung low and toxic over the city, exacerbated by drought, and she and Cobie had briefly left in search of cleaner air and richer feeding grounds. But finally the fires had been extinguished and cool breezes had swept away the pollution, and they'd returned to their home in this park.

This little island in the middle of the lake was the place Signet felt most safe. She and Cobie had raised several clutches of cygnets here, and the babies had grown up strong and healthy, and eventually headed off to find their own territory and create their own families.

And now, it was time to do it again. When Cobie returned with softer grasses, Signet stamped them into the mound, then gazed at him with gratitude. She was so glad they'd found each other, and discovered this park. And that they were still the only two swans in it.

Then she heard a familiar voice, and turned towards it.

"Where are the swans Daddy?" Gracie asked, peering anxiously around the lake.

Signet squeaked her intentions to Cobie, then glided across the water to greet her plucky little defender friend.

"Hello Signet Swan. I'm so glad you're back, because I've missed you," Gracie cooed, then she leaned in and whispered conspiratorially. "I love the ducks and the swamp hens too, but you are definitely my favourite."

Gently she reached out her hand, offering a bunch of fresh clover, and Signet nibbled it from her, making her laugh with delight at being tickled. Then Gracie pulled a bag from her dad's shoulder, filled with juicy cut grapes and green peas, the swan's favourites.

"I guess we should save some for your husband," she said eventually. "I'll just leave them in the shallows for him, if you want to let him know they're here."

Her father approached Gracie, his eyes softening as he looked at his daughter, then a fleeting glimpse of pain and fear flitted across his face before being hidden away. "We should go honey, your mum is getting cold."

Signet glanced up, wondering why he seemed so sad, then she spotted Gracie's mother, rugged up against the faint chill, a beanie on her closely cropped head, and her frame thinner and more fragile than last season. There were dark shadows under her eyes, and when she coughed, her whole body convulsed.

The next morning dawned chilly, but the sky was blue and the pale sun was shining, a perfect autumn day. In contrast to her mother, Gracie was a rosy-cheeked, loose-haired picture of health and vitality, enthusiasm sparkling in her eyes as she ran down the grassy bank, excited to see both swans waiting near the shore for her.

"Hello Mr and Mrs Swan," she grinned. "How is your nest building going? I can't wait to meet your new babies."

Crouching down, she gathered some fresh clover for them, but as she stood up, she saw a boy a bit further along the lake edge, throwing bread to the ducks. Gracie's brow furrowed. Gently she gave the leaves to the swans, murmured that she'd be back, then marched over to him, determination in every sharp angle of her body.

When she reached him though, she paused for a moment, suddenly shy. Signet watched her take a deep breath, summon her courage, then tap him on the shoulder, muttering to herself that it was for the animals.

"Excuse me?" she said, voice tentative.

The boy turned and regarded her coolly. "Yes?"

"Um, my name is Gracie, and I've been feeding the swans and the ducks here for years."

His mother's lips twitched, hiding a smile, but the little girl continued on.

"Well, the thing is, feeding any of the birds bread is really bad for them."

The boy stared at her, face sullen. "But they love it. They can't wait till I throw it to them. The ducks even fight for it."

"I didn't say they don't like it, just that it's bad for them. Like lollies are for us," Gracie said, a frown of concentration wrinkling her forehead. "I did a project at school about it. Their bodies can't process flour, sugar or yeast, so they get sick if they eat any. It can make them weak, and make them have unhealthy babies too. And if the babies eat lots of bread they get too big and fat for their little legs, and can no longer walk or fly. And if the bread is mouldy, it can even kill them."

The little boy gasped, and stared up at his mum with wide eyes. "Is that true?"

His mother was about to say no, when she noticed the sign tacked right in front of her. Quickly scanning it, she reluctantly nodded. "Yes, that does seem to be true."

She gazed down at Gracie. "I'm so sorry, I honestly didn't think about it."

Gracie smiled at her then turned to the boy. "There are things we can feed them, which they think are yummy, and are also good for them. Here, I have some, if you want to share them with me?"

The boy scowled, then finally nodded. "Thanks." He reached into her bag, and the two of them were soon giggling as they threw peas and corn and grape halves to the water birds.

When Cobie dipped his long neck underwater, the boy pointed at him. "What's it doing?"

"That's Cobie. He's nibbling on the roots and stems of the water weeds," Gracie replied. "Swans mostly eat greens – plants and algae, and grass and clover if they go waddling along the shore. And the babies sometimes eat bugs from on top of the water, because their necks aren't long enough yet to get to the reeds."

"That's fascinating," the boy's mother said. "You must really love swans."

Gracie nodded happily. "I do!"

"Thank you for telling us. I'll make sure we bring the right food next time. And thank you for sharing yours with Nicholas today."

Warmth suffused Signet, and she felt her heart expanding at the bravery of the little girl, who had been shaking with fear before she reprimanded the boy, but had done it anyway, making herself speak up, and doing it as kindly as she could. She was proud of the little boy and his mum too, for taking the lesson on board and vowing to do better.

That winter and spring the swan and her beloved thrived on the lake, bringing up their four new babies, and enjoying the treats Gracie brought them and the conversations she had with them. Although the little girl would be shocked if she knew that Signet understood every word she said.

Chapter 3

The following year when she returned to the lake after a brief time away, Signet was stunned to see the change in Gracie. She was following her dad down to the shore of the lake as usual, holding his hand, but there was no enthusiasm. She dragged her feet, and didn't even look up as they approached the water. Her dad handed her some peas, and she threw them into the lake without a care, not commenting when one of the swamp hens gobbled most of them up. And when a young boy threw bread to the ducks, Gracie barely even glanced at him.

What had happened to the sunny natured little girl? The one who so fiercely protected the wildlife in her local park, speaking up when people fed them the wrong food or threatened them in any way?

When Gracie's dad answered his phone and started arguing with someone, Signet paddled closer to try to hear what was going on.

"I can't just leave my daughter alone at a minute's notice and come in to the office," he said, pacing up and down. After a pause as he listened to the person on the other end of the line, his voice grew angry. "I'm sorry, but my wife died four months ago, as you well know, so I need to be with my daughter. I already work late every night, which is why I have a nanny all week, so I can't drop everything on a Saturday just because you want to do less work. I'll see you on Monday." And he hung up, then furiously punched in another number.

Signet's heart broke for Gracie. Her mother had died, which explained the change in her behaviour and mood. She was too young to have to deal with such a huge loss. Swimming closer, the swan gazed up at the little girl, then lifted her body, flapping her wings to gain height, and nudged her friend's hand.

"Oh, hello Mrs Swan," Gracie finally said, but her voice was devoid of emotion. "Sorry, I'm a bit distracted. Well, that's what my teacher says. But how have you been? Is your husband here too?"

Twisting her long, elegant neck, Signet indicated the island in the middle of the lake, where Cobie was sitting proudly on their nest of five eggs.

For a brief moment the joy returned to Gracie's face, and she clapped her hands in delight. "I can't wait to meet your babies. And I know you'll be a good mumma."

Her voice shook on the last word, and she covered her face with her hands and sobbed. But when her dad finally put his phone back in his pocket and came over to say they had to get home, Gracie pulled herself together, a mask slipping back on to hide her pain.

"Daddy, Signet and Cobie are going to have babies soon, so can we visit more often, and bring them some food?"

Her father looked surprised at her words, but nodded happily. "Of course we can darling," he said eagerly. "I didn't think you wanted to come back here. You said there were too many memories."

Shrugging, Gracie lapsed back into looking unconcerned and unenthused, but when she glanced at Signet again, she smiled. "Well, the swan family will need us, to make sure the other birds don't take all the food. And, um, can I just get Mrs Swan some clover before we go?"

As Gracie rushed off to pick the leaves, her father smiled at Signet. "Thank you Mrs Swan, you have no idea how grateful I am to you. That's the first genuine smile she's given me in the past four months. I'll bring you more peas than you could ever eat for this."

Father and daughter returned to the park the next day, with a mesh bag of peas and corn that Gracie distributed fairly between the swamp hens and ducks, before she called out to Signet and produced a second bag. "I saved you the best ones," she whispered proudly. "And there are some grapes too, cut in half, just the way you like them. Do you want some now, then you can take over on your nest and send Mr Swan over for his?"

Touched by the girl's thoughtfulness, Signet ate the food she offered, then swam back to her nest and told Cobie to go over and see Gracie.

When their cygnets were born a few weeks later, the little girl came every day after school, dragging a bored-looking older woman behind her, and running down the slope to ooh and ahh at the fuzzy grey babies.

"Oh Signet, they're so beautiful," she said. "And you are too. It makes me happy to see your little family together."

A shadow passed over Gracie's face, then she took a deep breath and focused back on the cygnets, giggling as she watched them tentatively nibble on the peas and spinach leaves she'd brought. When Cobie nipped at a swamp hen who was trying to take some of the food, she looked shocked for a moment, but then she told Signet she understood. "It's lovely that you're both so protective of your bubbas. You are very good parents."

Signet felt a rush of warmth for the little girl. Gracie was a fierce protector too, a feisty little guardian who brought them sustenance, and who was hawk-eyed and vigilant again if other children were offering the wrong food to the local wildlife. And she came to visit them even when it was raining, much to the despair of the woman who was always trailing her.

But one afternoon the nanny told her it was time to leave, and Gracie's face turned red with fury. She clenched her small hands into fists and glared at the woman.

"No! I'm not ready to go yet," she retorted, chin raised and arms crossed.

Somehow remaining calm in the face of the little girl's sudden hostility, the nanny smiled patiently. "Come on dear, it's time to get home and have a bath, then we can look at your homework while dinner cooks."

Gracie glared at her, rage sparking in her eyes. "You're not the boss of me. I don't have to do what you say."

"You do actually," the nanny said, still maintaining her cool manner and calm tone of voice, in spite of her charge's bad temper. "Come on, I know you're better behaved than this Gracie. Let's go now."

"No! I'm not going. I hate you!" Gracie shouted furiously. "You're not my mother!"

And she ran off around the lake, body rigid with defiance, eyes blinded by tears, until she tripped over and lay sprawled on the wet ground, crying now with physical pain as well as anger. Signet paddled closer, shocked by the little girl's out-of-character behaviour, and devastated by how sad and broken she obviously was.

Desperately she wished she could speak, could fold her in a hug and soothe her distress, but all she could do was watch, helpless, as the nanny made her way over to her and helped her to her feet, then led the sobbing child away.

It was a few days before Gracie returned to the park. Sheepishly she made her way down to the water's edge to talk to Signet, with her nanny watching on from a distance. "I'm so sorry Mrs Swan, that you had to see my outburst. And I hope I didn't scare your bubbas," she said, shame making her voice low. "I shouldn't still be having tantrums at my age, and I'll do my best not to have another one. I hope you can forgive me."

The swan lifted her head and nuzzled in close to Gracie. Of course she forgave her friend, and she understood that she was acting out because of her grief, and all the awful feelings she just couldn't contain, or explain.

"And I'm sorry if it upset you," the young girl continued earnestly. "I never want to do anything that will worry you, so I'll try to be better. I apologised to Mrs Donnelly too, just so you know. She made me feel terrible about it, but the next day she was okay with me, I think. I just hope she didn't tell Daddy how mean I was. I feel bad enough that you know how nasty I can be."

Reassured by Gracie's apology, and her calmer demeanour, the swan signalled to Cobie, who brought their babies over to say hello. Laughing with delight, the little girl crouched down so she could get closer to them, and tenderly distributed the treats she'd brought. "You guys really are the cutest little creatures I've ever seen," she squealed. "You're so fuzzy!"

For a while Gracie lost herself in their world, enchanted by every move the cygnets made and every squeak they uttered. And this time when the rain began to fall and the nanny called her, she leaned down and gave her swan friend one final pat, then walked meekly up the hill and took the older woman's hand.

Signet was relieved that Gracie had returned to her usual sweet nature, and glad she loved the cygnets as much as she and Cobie did. Her next few visits were uneventful, although the little girl always looked a little wistful when she referred to Signet as the swan mumma.

Life altered when the cygnets were three weeks old. The skies finally cleared, and strangers started coming to the park to see them and take photos. Most of them were curious yet respectful, and slightly awed by the five adorable balls of fluff. Yet there were a few visitors Cobie had to hiss at and scare away, especially those who brought their barking, biting dogs, which terrorised the cygnets and made the parent swans so anxious.

Three years ago, a dog had killed one of their babies, and Signet and Cobie had never forgotten it. And so they spent more and more time out on the island in the middle of the lake, where they could look after their little ones in peace, and keep them safe.

She trusted Gracie though, so whenever the little girl appeared, she swam the cygnets over to the shore and watched with great fondness as she giggled and gasped at how cute they were, and gently dropped the peas and corn she always brought into the shallows for them to eat.

One afternoon Gracie raced down to the water, cheeks flushed with excitement. "Signet, I've been watching your babies, seeing their personalities emerge, and thinking of names for them. How do you feel about Penny, Jacob, Siggy, Seth and Nessie?" She pointed each one out as she said the name, then looked at the mother swan, eyebrows raised in question. Signet inclined her head in agreement, hoping Gracie could sense her approval, and from then on she thought of her cygnets with those names too.

The little girl was the only person who could tell the baby swans apart, which thrilled Signet, and she was delighted that Gracie was deserving of the trust she and Cobie had granted her.

Chapter 4

Months passed, and the baby swans grew bigger and stronger. Gracie often came to visit, watching in awe as Cobie taught the youngsters to fly, and seeming just as sad as Signet when first Jacob and then Siggy flew away to find their own homes and start their own lives.

"Hello Mrs Swan," Gracie called out early one weekend morning. Then she peered around the lake. "Oh no, where's Nessie? Did she leave too? I'm so sorry, it must be hard for you to say goodbye."

Signet's eyes sparkled with joy, touched that her little friend had so quickly identified which of her children had left home, and grateful when she gathered a handful of juicy clover for her, then pulled out a small bag of peas. There was more food in the lake now, pond weeds and algae having bloomed with

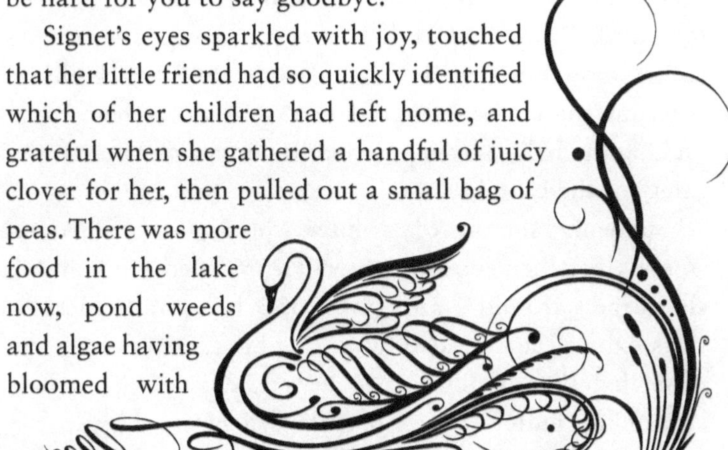

the recent rainfall, but she still loved the salad leaves, vegies and grapes Gracie brought her for a treat.

The little girl sighed, then wiped a tear from her eye. "If you were my mummy, I'd never leave you, I promise," she said. Her voice grew raspy as she tried to swallow down her distress. Signet swam closer, reaching her long neck up and nudging at the girl's hand, trying to offer some comfort. She'd seen the pain and naked longing on Gracie's face when she watched other children in the park with their two parents, and her heart hurt for her.

They had that in common, swan and human girl. The grief and sorrow of beloved family members lost to them, although Signet imagined Gracie's pain ran deeper than hers. At least she still had Cobie, and two of their cygnets.

When tragedy struck, it was a sweet spring day, the kind of day that usually lifts the heart with joy, promising sunshine and happiness ahead.

How misleading.

Gliding across the smooth, sparkling surface of the lake with Penny and Seth by her side, Signet noticed a rowdy crowd of boys playing a game close to the shore. Nervous about how aggressively a few of them were kicking the ball, she shepherded her offspring back to the safety of the island.

Suddenly she heard a huge splash, and a pained squawking, then loud laughter. Heart filled with dread, she turned around – and saw Cobie lying motionless in the shallows, surrounded by jeering boys. Desperately she propelled herself across the water between them, half swimming, half flying, and collapsed beside him in the clear green water.

Nudging his still body with her beak, her heart froze in terror when he didn't respond. What could she do? How could she help him?

Before she could think of anything, she sensed someone running towards them, and looked up in panic. But it was Gracie's dad, a worried frown on his face, not more brutish boys. Without stopping to take his shoes off, he waded into the water next to them, and gently lifted Cobie into his arms. Stroking his head, he leaned down to listen for a heartbeat, then apparently reassured that he was still breathing, pulled a phone from his pocket and punched in some numbers.

"Yes, hello. I'm in the park, and there's an injured swan. He's still breathing, but he seems to have been knocked unconscious, and his wing is at a strange angle…"

Impatiently he listened to the response, then spoke again. "Rough boys playing football. Seems one of them hit the swan on purpose… No, they've all gone now… That's fine, I'll wait here until you can get to us."

And he hung up, then gazed at Signet with tears shimmering in his eyes.

"I'm so sorry someone did this Mrs Swan. I'm sure he'll be okay though," he said gently.

She didn't know if he was trying to convince her, or himself. He sank down heavily on the bank, not caring that his shoes and pants were wet and muddy, and cradled Cobie in his arms.

Then he looked up in alarm. "Do you mind me holding him? I'm so sorry, I didn't even ask you."

Signet tilted her head to one side and regarded him. She could sense his kindness, so she tried to nod, tried to convey to him that she trusted him enough to hold her beloved.

A moment later, Gracie came running down the hill – and gasped in horror when she saw the fallen swan in her father's arms.

"What happened Daddy?" Her voice trembled with sorrow, and again Signet wished she could comfort her.

"There were some thoughtless boys playing football, much too close to the lake and all the birds. One of them hit the swan with the ball."

"That's so horrible. Nasty boys!" She stamped her foot angrily, then took a deep breath and spoke more softly. "Will Cobie be okay?"

For a moment her father hesitated, then he made his voice sound strong. "Yes, I think he will be absolutely fine. The wildlife volunteers are on their way, and they'll be able to help him. I'm sure he'll regain consciousness soon, and the injury to his wing will heal in time. It will be tricky for him until then though."

Gracie's bottom lip wobbled, but she managed to calm herself down. She turned to Signet. "I'm sorry they were mean to you, and hurt your husband. Are Penny and Seth all right? Are you?"

Mind whirring, Signet turned to the other side of the lake, where she'd left their cygnets. They must be panicking over what they'd seen. Then she stared back at Cobie. She wasn't sure where to go or who to be with.

"This one's okay with us for the moment, if you want to go and check on your babies," Gracie's dad said.

Knowing Cobie was in good hands, she sped back across the lake, hurried and not as graceful as usual. Drawing her little ones close to her, she guided them back over towards Cobie, reassuring them that all would be well in time.

She hoped.

It was an hour before the wildlife officer turned up, but Gracie and her dad had stayed with the swans, making sure no one else approached, and tenderly stroking Cobie's head. The little girl kept up her conversation with Signet, her own sadness forgotten, or at least pushed down and hidden away, while she tried to comfort her bird friend.

When the man in khaki appeared, he thanked Gracie and her dad, then gently lifted Cobie onto a makeshift stretcher and prepared to leave.

"What will happen to him?" Gracie asked, fear making her voice shake.

The man smiled at her. "We'll take him to the animal hospital and they'll make him better. With any luck he'll be back here swimming around the lake in no time."

There was relief on Gracie's face, and Signet was overjoyed to hear this too – until she saw the look the wildlife carer exchanged with the little girl's father.

Oh no.

Chapter 5

The next time Signet saw Gracie, a few weeks later, she turned up after school with a new, much younger, companion, and walked listlessly down to the water's edge on her own. The teenager took a seat at one of the picnic tables, phone in hand, eyes glued to the screen, and totally ignored the girl in her charge. Signet stared at her, alarmed. She hadn't even glanced at the lake, or any of the other potential dangers facing a child in the park. Who was she? Where was Mrs Donnelly?

Signet knew Gracie was sensible, but if that teenager was supposed to be looking after her, she should be paying attention. And why was Gracie so sad today? She could see her own grief mirrored in the girl's slumped shoulders and her tear-stained eyes, and her heart ached for her little friend.

"Oh, hello Mrs Swan," Gracie said, when she finally noticed how close the graceful bird had come. "I'm sorry I'm not very good company, I'm too upset. Mrs Donnelly quit, because apparently my tantrum was too much for her to handle, and Daddy is really mad at me."

The little girl sighed like she had the weight of the whole world on her shoulders, then she tried to pull herself together, forcing a brief smile. "I did bring you some peas though. How are you going?"

Gently dropping some of the vegies in the shallows, Gracie gazed around the lake, then gasped in horror. "Has your husband not come back yet?"

Signet let her head drop, dejected, and Gracie reached out a hand to pat her.

"I'm so sorry Mrs Swan. And oh my gosh, have Penny and Seth gone too?"

The swan emitted a mournful cry, and her friend frowned. "It's not fair that you're alone as well. You're probably the only one who understands how I feel, because you've lost your family too."

Gracie's eyes glistened with unshed tears, which she angrily wiped away. "I miss my mummy so much. Why did she have to die? And Daddy seems to have disappeared too. He just works all the time. Some nights he doesn't even get home in time to tuck me in. So I'm left with Ingrid."

She jerked her thumb towards the girl still hunched over her phone. "She's not mean to me or anything, and we don't have fights like I did with the last one, but that's because she doesn't care about me at all. At least Mrs Donnelly was concerned about me, when I wasn't being naughty."

Shoulders slumping, Gracie swallowed down a sob. "Ingrid doesn't spend any time with me, like she's supposed to. Reading to me, or playing, or helping with my homework. When we're out she's glued to her phone, even walking to school, and it's the same at home, she just switches on the telly for me then goes back to her phone, or if her boyfriend comes over, ignores me completely. I'm so bored Mrs Swan, and so sad and lonely."

Tears trembled on Gracie's lashes, and Signet wished she could step out of the water and enfold the girl in a hug. Gently she leaned in closer, nudging her hand, wanting so badly to comfort her and make her feel better.

Gracie smiled and stroked her swan friend's soft head. "Thank you for listening to me. I'm trying to be brave, and not stress Daddy out, but I'm worried about him too. When I do see him, he just looks at me and cries. Is he mad at me? I don't understand. I don't know what I did wrong." Her voice was strangled and broken, and the tears she'd been controlling so bravely finally spilled over her lashes and cascaded down her cheeks.

The little girl's pain was so visceral that Signet felt the deep rumbling of it within her own body. It swirled through her, amplifying her own sorrow and unlocking a hidden well of empathy that was particularly unswanlike.

Desperately she tried to think of something she could do to help her friend. Gracie shouldn't be so thoroughly ignored by her new nanny, and she couldn't be left to think that her father was angry with her either. That wasn't fair, when she was already so broken by grief and loss. But what could a swan do to help a human?

The honk of an ibis sounded across the lake, and Signet whipped her head around to stare at it. She remembered the wisp of a story she'd heard from one of the ibises, of a pelican transforming into a man to save a little boy's life. Gracie's need wasn't as dramatic as that, but if *she* could turn into a human, even for a day, she would treat the little girl so much better than everyone else in her life seemed to. Would listen to her, and comfort her, and lavish attention and love on her.

"I'm sorry Mrs Swan, I shouldn't be complaining to you, because you have your own troubles." Gracie smiled bravely, and wiped at her eyes, but a single tear ran down her face and dropped into the water. Signet stared at the ripples radiating outward from it. It couldn't really be true, could it, that drinking a human tear would transform a bird into a person?

Amused by her own her gullibility, the swan bent her long neck towards the surface, dipped her beak in, and swallowed the tear before it sank to the bottom of the lake.

Then she waited.

She tried to smile at Gracie, tried to offer a sign that she would help her, would look after her, but nothing happened. No change. She felt exactly the same. And what had she expected, really? A swan could no sooner turn into a human as lead could transform into gold, and how many foolish people had fallen for the latter dream over the centuries?

Feeling ridiculous for believing it could have worked, Signet ducked her head in embarrassment, and turned away to swim back across the lake.

Suddenly a shiver vibrated through her body. Her vision blurred, and she blinked rapidly, trying to see through the mist that was swirling around her. Then her face stiffened. Her whole body became icy cold, then her temperature spiked, as though it was noon of the hottest summer day on record, rather than the mild spring early evening cool that was settling over the park.

Her head spun. Was something happening after all?

Scared, the swan tried to get Gracie's attention, but everything was in slow motion, like she was under water. Was she? Peering ahead, Signet could just make out her friend, but the little girl's body was swaying, like a pond weed in the lake.

That couldn't be right.

Dimly she heard the teenager, Ingrid, calling Gracie's name, and as the light faded around Signet, she was aware, on the edge of her consciousness, that the small girl was bidding her farewell and blowing her a kiss. Surely she wouldn't go home and leave her all alone here if there was something wrong with her, so she must be okay, right?

Was she dreaming then? Was this just a strange hallucination brought on by the shock of her own grief, and the wishful thinking that she could help her friend?

Would all of this strangeness dissipate as soon as she could force her eyes open again and wake up?

Chapter 6

For a while Signet drifted, disassociating from the pain rippling through her body, wondering if this was what death was, and if so, whether she would meet her beloved in the Otherworld. She smiled at the thought, and willed her spirit towards it. Her eyes grew filmy, and the world around her darkened as she prepared to float away.

Yet something was holding her to life, to the earth, to this park on the edge of the city where she had been so happy and felt so safe.

There was the physical distress trapping her where she was, but also the memory of a sweet little girl who had fed and protected Signet and her family for so long, even when her own heart was breaking, and the vow the swan had made to help her.

Filled with new determination, Signet willed

herself back into her body, struggling not to flinch as the agony rolled through her again. Breathing deeply, she focused on Gracie's face, which calmed her a little, then tried to picture Cobie, gliding across the lake towards her, helping her build their nest, sitting devotedly on their eggs for hours and hours at a time. The thought lifted her spirits, and the memory of their love helped her to endure.

When the sun finally set and night fell over the park, Signet shook herself, trying to soothe her aching muscles, to relieve the painful tearing she felt within her very being. Gingerly, she stretched her neck upwards and extended her wing – then stared in total shock as it elongated and slowly revealed itself as a human arm. Her legs had lengthened and thickened too, and as she stumbled out of the shallows at the edge of the lake, she lifted the long cloak of black swan feathers that was swamping her above the water, marvelling at the softness of the garment, and the way the wind ruffled through the downy material.

Then she gasped. Beneath it, peeking out from the black feathers, she saw human skin. Suddenly feeling exposed, she clutched the cloak more tightly around herself, and gazed nervously around the park.

She was wobbly on her new legs, and vulnerable. Sometimes, as night fell, revellers came to this park, drinking out of glass bottles, laughing too loudly, lurching as they walked, and sometimes falling over. On a few occasions fights had broken out, and she was terrified that one of these men would find her before she'd grown into her new body. She was like a cygnet just hatching from its egg, clumsy and bewildered, stumbling on unsteady feet with no clue where to go, or what to do.

She still couldn't believe it had actually happened.

The sharp trilling cackle of a kookaburra pierced the silence. Her glance slid abruptly in that direction, and she squinted through strange blurry eyes until she made out the bird perched on the branch of a tree. And in the shadows below it, almost invisible in the darkness despite its long white-feathered cloak, stood a figure. He beckoned to her, and she staggered towards him on shaky legs, almost losing her balance and falling over several times.

"Signet."

The voice was a whisper on the wind, a gentle breeze, wrapping around her and comforting her. Lending strength to her wobbly legs, opening her mind to a more human perspective. She shivered. Who was he? *What* was he?

She gazed at the figure, taking in the long grey hair and beard, the soft black velvet hat that sat low on his brow, and the pale, feathery cloak that seemed to hold all the starlight of the night sky within it. His eyes twinkled just as brightly, and she relaxed a little.

"I can feel your sadness Signet, as well as your love and compassion for the little girl who has always been so kind to you. And who has suffered her own loss, just like you."

At his words, her heart hurt even more sharply than before. Her knees buckled, and she swayed. Human emotions were rawer. More intense. She wasn't sure she could handle the weight of this pain, her grief intensified a hundredfold.

Gracie must be a complete mess.

The man's hand shot out to steady her. "Your motives are pure, but are you sure you're up to the task? It will be difficult. Challenging." He stared at her, his eyes hooded, ancient, and she thought of the ibis she'd heard the tale of transformation from. Was this him?

He raised an eyebrow, and his mouth quirked up on one side, but he continued speaking. "Becoming a human will take a toll on you Signet, on your body and your mind. And I must warn you that you will be stuck here, in this form. There is no going back. If you choose to do this, you will be forever a woman. You can't ever return to your swan form, no matter what, and you can't tell anyone what you once were either. You will live longer as a human, but it will be tougher. More painful."

Images flashed before her eyes, too fast to properly comprehend, but leaving an impression of the strangeness of the world she would be entering. Dangerous. Confusing. Precarious. Painful. Lonely.

But what was the alternative? Watch the poor little girl cry every day? See her eaten up with pain and bitterness and hate, shouting angry words at people, when she'd always been such a kind soul? She couldn't let that happen, not if she had a chance to help her.

"I am prepared to do it." Slowly she experimented with the words, swirling them around in her new mouth. Her voice sounded raw. Ragged. Nothing at all like Gracie's, or her father's. She may be willing, but was she capable of this? Would they even understand what she was saying to them? And how would she know what to do? Where would she go? How would she find them?

There was no way she could do this.

What did she know about human love anyway? Would she even be able to help Gracie, with her limited swan emotions, or would she make things worse? And what if Cobie returned to the park in search of her? She would never forgive herself if she couldn't get back to him. If she left him all alone.

Panic gripped her. No. She couldn't risk losing her beloved. She couldn't go through with this.

"Wait!"

But the man was nodding. If there had been a test, she'd somehow made it through. And if there had been a chance to back out, it had passed. It was too late.

"Very well. In this bag you will find clothes, information, a letter of introduction and keys to your apartment – everything you will need to slip into your new world."

He stared at her, and she saw the shadows under his eyes, the anguish etched into his face. "I won't lie Signet, it hurts to be a human, emotionally as well as physically. You will ache with loss, grieve over what can never be, and cry at the tragedy of the world." Then he paused, and smiled.

"But it is wonderful too. Humans are compassionate and caring, creative and inventive. They cause so many problems, but they can solve them too. And to live each day with the potential to help another person, to experience the kindness of strangers, is something else. To feel your heart soar amongst the stars with a love that transcends time and space, a yearning that inspires poetry and music and art, every facet of the imagination you can dream up? It's Otherworldly. The tenderness of the human spirit will transform you, and transport you. That's the reason for the pain, I think – for you cannot have light without dark, or joy without sorrow."

There was a fluttering in Signet's stomach. Her heart raced, and her legs shook. What on earth had she gotten herself into? "How will I know what to do?"

The wizened old man reached out and lifted her chin. "I have faith in you."

Then he faded away into the shadows and was gone.

Chapter 7

Dropping down onto her haunches, still clutching the black-feathered cloak around her naked body, Signet unzipped the bag, and smiled. There was a dress in it, blue like the surface of the lake, and long and loose enough to shelter her, and hide her discomfort in this new physical form. She slipped it over her head, then gently folded her cloak and placed it in the bag.

Her fingers touched paper, and she pulled out a large white envelope and slid it open. Inside was a detailed map showing the park and the lake and the trees, with an X on the spot where she now stood. A path was marked that climbed the hill before her, then continued onwards from there. There was a smaller envelope too, with a name scrawled across the front in small black letters – Daniel Pennington – along with a set of keys and a thick green book called *How To Be Human*.

Running a shaking hand through her long black hair, Signet flipped through the first few pages, overwhelmed by all the instructions, rules, lists, maps and pictures. Would this be enough to help her fake being a real person?

Following the words with her finger, she tried to make sense of them, but a loud laugh and drunken jeering carried to her on the wind, and she panicked. She couldn't face an encounter with human strangers right now, especially if they'd been drinking.

Heart racing in her chest, she almost tore the dress off her body and retreated back into her cloak of feathers, into the safety of her watery world. But the voice of the old man – the Ibis Man? – echoed in her head.

"You will be stuck here…"

"There is no going back."

"You will be forever a woman."

She gulped, and saw a flash of her beloved Cobie, gone for two full lunar cycles now. What if he returned to the park and couldn't find her?

What had she done?

Her fear of the unknown rose, nearly paralysing her, but it was too late to back out. Recalling the pain in Gracie's sad eyes, she focused on the devastated little girl she wanted to help, and let that give her the strength to throw everything back in the bag, zip it closed and move forward.

Climbing the hill on still-weak legs, she gazed up at the full moon and whispered a prayer of hope and a desperate plea for the wisdom she would need to play her new role.

At the summit she stopped abruptly, startled by the strange rumbling noise of different coloured machines whizzing past down below, and the searing illumination of tiny suns trapped in glass balls overhead, which showed her the way down the darkening path ahead of her. As she descended the hill, the noise grew louder, and she wanted to scurry back to the tranquil safety of the lake and hide. But curiosity, and an awful feeling of inevitability that sat like a stone in her stomach, compelled her onwards, towards the strange black river with fast, noisy boats gliding along the surface.

Suddenly an arm shot out and grabbed her, and she jumped in fright.

"Wait! Are you trying to get yourself killed?" a voice shrieked, and she stared around herself in confusion. The coloured lights and speeding vehicles were disorientating her, and she gazed at the stranger in panic. The voice implied danger, and she tensed, trying to identify whatever was threatening her. There were no foxes in the middle of the city though, were there?

"Are you all right?" The voice softened, more sympathetic now, and she nodded quickly. She had to get it together.

"Okay, the light is green for us now, so we can cross the road," the man said, indicating that she should walk next to him. With great trepidation, she allowed him to lead her across the wide black river. It was confusing. The surface was hard, not watery at all. A few times she and Cobie had flown over here on their way north, but from their height she'd assumed it was a smaller stream.

Realising the man was still speaking, she tried to focus, to comprehend. "When the light's red, you have to stop and wait, or you'll be hit by a car." He frowned at her. "Are you sure you're okay? Are you new here?"

Numbly she nodded, and continued to put one foot in front of the other. "Yes," she croaked, startling herself with the sound of the word she'd managed to utter.

"Good. Well, I go this way. Look after yourself." And he was gone, swallowed up by the night.

Clutching the bag to her chest, Signet stood under a glowing ball of light and tried to figure out what to do. How was she supposed to find Gracie? Why hadn't she asked Ibis Man to tell her that, at least? Was she supposed to wander the streets aimlessly until she stumbled across her? It was night-time now, the stars blocked out by all the fake golden lights, so Gracie probably wouldn't leave her house until she had to go to school in the morning.

Shivering with fear and dread, Signet stared at the speeding cars and flashing lights. Would it be safer to spend the night in the park, despite the loud men who scared her?

The map. Setting her bag down, she retrieved the sheet of paper and tried to figure out where she was now she'd left the familiarity of her lake and its surrounds. Her fingernails bit into her palms as she balled her fists, and tears of frustration welled in her eyes. Fear swirled around her like feathers, close and choking, a living thing she wasn't sure she could deal with.

She was just about to give up and return to the safety of her home, when she heard a familiar voice.

Gracie's father.

"Wait, Ingrid, what do you mean you're leaving now, with no notice at all? I can't just find someone to watch Gracie out of thin air!"

The sullen teenager shrugged and muttered something Signet couldn't hear. Quickly she moved towards them, the small envelope in her hand, along with the keys.

"Hello," she said, voice still croaky. Did she sound like a human, or a baby frog?

Gracie's dad swung around to face her, and his eyes widened.

"Um, do I know you?" he asked, not unkindly, brow furrowed in consternation.

She shook her head, trying to remember the instructions Ibis Man had given her, and the notes in the book. "No, but the agency said you might need someone to take your daughter to school in the mornings, then pick her up afterwards and watch her until you get home from work."

Nervously she handed over the envelope, hoping it was for him, and waited, breath held, while he opened it and scanned the contents of the letter.

When his mouth dropped open in astonished joy, she exhaled in relief.

"This is perfect. Signet, is it?"

She nodded. She supposed the name Gracie had given her was as good as any other.

"So perfect," Gracie's dad said, jolting her back to the present. "When can you start?"

"Oh. Um, tomorrow?"

"You're a lifesaver," he said. "Where do you live?"

Wordlessly she held out her keys, the number writ large on a white plastic tag, a grey fob next to it.

He grinned. "This is like magic! What are the odds that you would be available right when I need you, and live in an apartment downstairs from me and Gracie? It's almost too good to be true. Are you my faery godmother?"

Shrugging helplessly, Signet tried to figure out what he meant. She'd never heard the term, and none of the faeries she knew had mothers.

"So, I can go now?" Ingrid asked impatiently, and Gracie's dad nodded, too distracted to even bid her farewell.

"Oh this is wonderful Signet, you have no idea. So you can take Gracie to school tomorrow?"

Tilting her head to the side as she gazed at him, she wished she knew the answer. Could she do this?

Finally she nodded.

"Do you know where the school is?"

Panic gripped her again, but when she looked down at her map, she saw a thin red line moving from where they stood at the intersection, continuing along the road before turning left, then taking another right. A small X seemed to mark the location.

"Yes." Her voice still sounded strange in her ears, but Gracie's dad didn't seem to notice anything untoward.

Smiling, he extended his hand, and she shook it, grateful that she'd observed someone do that in the park recently. "And sorry, I'm Daniel, in case I was too overwhelmed with relief to tell you that earlier."

"Hello Daniel."

He was grinning as he shepherded her across another road and towards the entrance to a large building.

Leading her into a strange cubicle, he pressed the number two button, and the doors shut. With a jolt, the small room they were in started moving them upwards. When the doors opened again, there was a long corridor stretching off to her right, and Daniel led her out and along the hall, before stopping at a door with a number on it.

"Here you are, apartment 6-28. Gracie and I are on the fifth floor, directly above you, number 6-58." His eyes sparkled with relief, and more joy than she'd noted in him for a long time. "So, we'll see you at eight?"

Signet nodded, then watched him walk away, leaving her alone in the dimly lit hallway. With a deep breath to try to steady her racing pulse, she put the key in the lock, fumbling until she figured it out, then opened the door.

A switch next to it made the room light up, and she took in the bench and the sinks to her right, the table and chairs ahead of her, the couch along the far wall, and two rooms off to the side.

Flicking through her guidebook, she searched for the apartment instructions. So, she was standing in the kitchen, with the lounge and dining areas in front of her, and those two doors would be to the bedroom and the bathroom. She'd explore them later.

First, she opened the big white box in the kitchen, and gasped in astonishment at all the shelves filled with different greens. There were bowls of peas, spinach leaves, lettuce, a container of grapes, some yellow corn kernels, and green apples. All the foods Gracie would bring her for a treat. Trying to ground herself, she nibbled on some grapes while she gazed around the place.

A bead of sweat trickled between her shoulder blades, her skin turned cold and clammy, and her heart raced with terror. Being locked inside a building, when she was so used to the freedom of the lake and the open sky above her, was freaking her out. She swore under her breath, using all the words she'd heard in the park over the years.

She couldn't do this.

Her body ached, tears welled in her eyes, and her mind was a jagged mess of black thoughts, chaos and swirling fears. Despite the guidebook, she had absolutely no idea how to be a human. Darkness closed in around her, and she slumped to the floor.

Chapter 8

Signet's eyes snapped open. A terrible buzzing kept ringing in her ears, making her head hurt. Confused, she looked wildly around herself, trying to work out what it was, and how to stop it.

Work out where she was.

Work out what she was.

She shrieked as she saw the four walls around her, felt a hard floor beneath her aching body, comprehended the dimness of the light, and the absence of blue sky above her.

Memories tumbled back to her as she dragged herself to her feet.

Memories of Gracie crying at the lake, and Signet dipping her beak into the water and drinking the little girl's tear so she could transform into a human and help her.

Memories of herself actually transforming.

Fear made Signet dizzy, and she reached blindly for the wall. She hadn't believed it would work, not really, yet here she was, standing helpless in a human apartment, in a human body, about to start a human job.

Panicked, she opened one of the two closed doors and peered into what must be the bedroom, and finally discovered the small box that was making the noise. She smacked her hand down on top of it, and mercifully the blaring that was drilling into her brain stopped.

Flopping onto the bed, she sighed at how comfortable it was. Last night she'd been so overwhelmed, so exhausted, that she hadn't even looked in this room, let alone made it to the bed, and the throbbing pain in her strange human limbs was making her regret that decision.

Reluctantly she stood up again, and gingerly opened the second door. The room was pale green, with a bath that she longed to fill to the brim and sink down into. But she didn't have time to soak in the soothing water. She had to pick Gracie up and take her to school.

Could she do this?

Retrieving her bag from the kitchen, she returned to the purple-painted bedroom. There was a wardrobe with an open door, and a row of dresses in various colours inside, so she pulled one on over her head, then headed back to the fridge for some grapes and spinach leaves.

It boggled her mind that Ibis Man had somehow magicked all of this into existence. A furnished apartment close to Gracie, filled with food and clothes and everything else she would need, including that annoying alarm clock. She tried to focus on the magic, because she was too scared to think beyond today, to wonder where she would get more food from when this ran out, or how she would pay for... whatever humans had to pay for.

Her pulse quickened as a rising terror threatened to swamp her, but she swallowed it down, grabbed her key, and hurried out the door and back down the hallway.

The strange box she'd arrived in the night before opened when she pushed the button, and she timidly made her way inside. A man was already in there, a folded newspaper under his arm, and he raised his eyebrows at her. "What number?"

She stared at him helplessly.

His eyes flicked to the panel next to the door. "Which floor are you on?"

"Oh!" She racked her brain. What had Daniel said? *Gracie and I are on the fifth floor, above you, number 6-58.*

"The fifth floor!" she said, proud to have remembered. She watched as he pushed the number five, then smiled at him. "Thank you."

He nodded absently, then peered at his paper. Clearly she didn't seem so strange and out of place that he was concerned by her presence, which was a relief. A little of the stress she'd been weighed down by slipped from her shoulders, and she headed cheerfully down the hallway to Gracie's flat.

The door opened just as she lifted her hand to knock, and Daniel stared at her in consternation.

"Good morning Signet," he said, then grinned. "Gracie said you were here, but I didn't believe her. Seems she's already on your wavelength." He lowered his voice conspiratorially. "I don't think she liked Ingrid, the last nanny, but I have a feeling you two are going to get along just fine."

"Daddy, was I right?" Gracie called out, then barrelled into the room and threw her arms around Signet's waist. "I was!" She beamed at the woman standing in the doorway. "I had a dream about you last night, and in it we were great friends. I'm very happy to meet you. Will you come to the park with me after school?"

"Yes, of course, whatever you'd like," Signet said, overwhelmed by the soothing warmth of the girl's embrace.

Daniel smiled at them, then leaned down to kiss his daughter goodbye. "You be good for Signet, please, and don't talk her ear off right away." Standing back up, he stretched out his hand and took Signet's. "Thank you so much for being available at such short notice, you have no idea how grateful I am. Would you like me to pay you into your bank account, or would you prefer cash?"

She stared at him, bewildered. *Bank account?*

"For your money. How would you like me to pay you? The letter of recommendation didn't say."

"Oh, um, cash would be great if that's all right?"

"Anything for you, I promise! You've really saved me so much grief. Now, I'll see you both tonight, okay? Bye!"

And he was gone, leaving Signet alone with Gracie. Who she felt like she knew, even though, in this alien human form, she was a complete stranger to the little girl. Anxiously she looked down at her.

"It's a pleasure to meet you Gracie, my name's Signet."

"Like the swan," Gracie said, giggling.

Signet stared at her in horror. How did she know her secret? "What do you mean?"

"Baby swans are called cygnets," her new charge said. "I'm friends with the swans in the park across the road, a really sweet married couple, and I've met some of their babies over the years," she said proudly. "I named the mumma swan Signet, and she is so lovely."

A wave of emotion washed over the swan maiden, and she wished she could tell Gracie how much she'd always appreciated her kindness and attention. "I bet that swan family loves you very much."

Gracie beamed at her, then took her hand and drew her further inside. "I know we have to go soon, but can I show you my room first?"

Swept up in the little girl's enthusiasm, Signet followed her down a short hallway to a light-filled room that had been painted sky blue, with trees stencilled on the walls, and a lake just near the bed. A lake that had two swans swimming peacefully on it. Signet's heart pounded and her stomach twisted. The longing she felt for Cobie was like a knife in her heart.

"Is that the swan couple?" she asked faintly.

Gracie frowned, and a shadow crossed her face. "Yes, but a terrible thing happened a couple of months ago."

She gulped, seeming reluctant to continue, but she eventually took up the story again. "Cobie, that's the daddy swan, he was hurt by some boys playing football. My daddy called the wildlife rescue people, and a man came to check on him. He said he would take Cobie to the animal hospital, and promised they would make him all better and he'd be back really soon. But he never returned. And I just feel so sad for his wife, who's all alone now."

It was a challenge for Signet not to break down in tears at her words. "Should we try to contact the wildlife rescue people, and find out what happened to him, and where he is now?" she asked tentatively, then held her breath, terrified, as she waited for the answer.

The little girl's eyes were as tear-filled as Signet's, and she paused before struggling on. "Daddy did call them, a few times, but they said the carer who found Cobie no longer works there, and they can't find any of the paperwork about his treatment or where he is now." A tear trickled down her cheek. "They don't even know if he's still alive, but I hope he is, and that he can find his way back to his wife."

The words, so gently delivered, were a savage blow. Signet staggered under the weight of them, collapsing onto the small bed.

"Are you okay?" Gracie asked solemnly.

The swan maiden made herself smile, although it came out as a grimace. "Um, yes, of course. Sorry sweetie, don't worry about me. I didn't mean to alarm you. I love your room by the way, and the mural is gorgeous."

Gracie's smile was just as forced. "Mummy painted it for me, just before she died. That was nearly a year ago now. The park is my happy place," she said, then a frown of despair and anger marred her delicate features. "I feel close to her there, because we used to go together all the time. And when I talk to the mumma swan, I feel like I'm talking to my mum."

A shiver of guilt curled up Signet's spine. Had she destroyed Gracie's last link to her mother by transforming into human form? Was she going to harm her more than she could actually help by being here?

A sob broke her reverie, and she felt Gracie collapse into her arms. She stroked her back, murmuring words of comfort, but she felt so helpless. Had she done the right thing coming here, slipping off her swan feathers and walking the world as a human?

"Thank you Signet," Gracie whispered when her tears finally stopped. "I could never cry in front of Ingrid, since she made me feel so stupid if I did, and I try really hard not to break down when Daddy's around too, because it just upsets him. Thanks for letting me be sad."

Horrified by the little girl's admission, Signet pushed her own worries to the back of her mind. There was definitely a lot she could do here to help. "You can be sad, and cry, any time you need to," she said gently. "I know what it's like to lose a loved one. It's like part of your soul is missing, and you're just half a... person." She'd almost said swan. She had to be careful.

But Gracie was staring up at her, eyes still swimming with tears, yet the corners of her lips raised slightly in an almost-smile. "Yes, that's it exactly. I'm so glad you're here, but I'm so sorry you've lost someone too," she said, reaching out a hand to pat Signet's arm. "Maybe we can help each other."

"Yes, I think we will," Signet said, smiling through her own tears. She rose unsteadily to her feet. "Now I guess we should make your lunch and get you to school, right?"

Chapter 9

Traffic sped by, horns blared, a siren roared, and chaos ruled, drowning out the gentle peace of the birds twittering in the treetops. Walking to school, it was Signet clutching Gracie's hand tightly in fear, not the other way around. She yearned for the tranquillity of her lake, realising how much the park was an oasis of calm in an otherwise frenetic city. The noise of the human world was going to take a long time to get used to.

Gracie's chatter kept her grounded though, and she focused on her charge, trying to shut out all the bright, flashing distractions, and her devastation at the news about Cobie. She realised now that she'd been clinging to the possibility, however slim, that he would somehow return to their lake. Now, the weight of that hope being crushed was threatening to drown her. But she had to bury her pain for now. She was here for Gracie.

When they finally made it to the school, Signet breathed a sigh of relief, until the young girl tugged on her arm and looked up at her with a pleading expression. "Will you come in with me, and meet my teacher?" she begged.

Signet blanched. Could she fool another woman? Would she give herself away? And what would she *say* to the teacher? But she pulled herself together and nodded. It was her job to make Gracie happy, so she reluctantly followed her across the yawning abyss of the playground into the huge grey building, then up a flight of stairs.

Hovering nervously at the doorway to the classroom, she watched as Gracie charged inside and spoke to the teacher, then took a seat at one of the small desks.

The teacher frowned at Signet, then rose to her feet and made her way over to the door.

"Good morning Miss Henwood, I'm Signet," the swan maiden said, anxiety making her voice shake. "It's lovely to meet you. Um, I'll be bringing Gracie to school each morning, and picking her up, while her father is so busy with work."

"Please, call me Janine," the teacher said, looking her up and down with a critical eye that belied her friendly voice. "Daniel called me last night to let me know you'd be here. Which is alarmingly fast, don't you think? Not even a chance to check your references."

Signet's mouth dropped open in shock, and butterflies fluttered wildly in her stomach. She hadn't expected to be best friends with the teacher, but her hostility was baffling.

"Still, I'm glad Ingrid is gone," Janine continued frostily. "She was a nice enough girl, but so young, and a little too preoccupied with her own life, I found. I hope *you're* not like that. Gracie needs stability in her life. Someone to care about her."

Biting her tongue, Signet forced a smile, and tried not to take the comments personally. The teacher was just looking out for her student, and she should be glad of that. "You have no need to worry Miss Henwood, I'm completely devoted to her and her wellbeing," she replied softly. "Gracie is my only focus."

"Hmm."

Time slowed, and Signet stood frozen, the teacher's judgement pouring over her in waves. If this meeting was a test, she was starting to worry that she'd failed. Would Janine call Daniel and have her fired?

Then, abruptly, the teacher changed tack.

"How is Daniel coping?" she asked, her voice softer, almost gentle. Signet was surprised to see the other woman's frosty eyes widen and a faint blush colour her cheeks.

"He's all right, though he's burying himself in work as a way to cope. And I know how much he loves his daughter, but sometimes it hurts him to be with her, because she is so much like his wife."

Janine's eyebrows rose in surprise, and Signet wondered where her words had come from. She recalled Gracie's mum's sweet face, so much like her daughter's, and Gracie's lament – was it only yesterday in the park? – that her dad seemed to be avoiding her, and that when she did see him, he just looked at her and cried. She knew how much Daniel loved her, so what else could it be?

"That's a remarkably astute observation for someone so new to the family," the teacher said, and there was resentment in her tone.

"I have been around children and their parents all my life," Signet replied. An image of the cruel boy and his cruel father flitted into her mind, and she grimaced. "These two love each other very much."

Reassured, Janine finally managed a smile. "Yes, Gracie was blessed to have two parents who adore her. And while I know Daniel is preoccupied, there is no doubting his protective instincts for his daughter. They remind me of swans actually, of the family in the local park that Gracie is always talking about. So loving and loyal, and protective of each other and their babies."

"Swans?" Signet gasped, panic rising. Could someone have told this woman what she was?

Janine laughed. "Gracie had us all involved in her project last term – she chose to study swans. She said there was a family in the park across the road from her, and she loved being there, and chatting to them. Not that she's… you know, off in a fantasy world or anything," she added quickly, clearly worried about giving the wrong impression. "She knows they can't understand her, but she really loves them, and they give her some comfort, which I'm grateful for."

A warm glow enveloped Signet, and she glanced into the classroom, waving when she saw Gracie gazing at her with curiosity sparkling in her green eyes.

"So what will you do for the rest of the day, until you have to pick Gracie up?" the teacher asked, her sudden friendliness jolting Signet back to the present, and her strange new reality. She had more than six hours to fill in, and the day stretched yawning and sad before her.

"Um, I'm not sure actually. Perhaps I'll go and walk through the park, see if I can chat with those swans."

A loud bell rang, making Signet jump, and Janine turned towards the classroom. "Sorry, I must get to work," she said abruptly. "I'll see you this afternoon." And she was gone, the door shut firmly in Signet's face.

Sadness engulfed the swan maiden as she wandered back towards her apartment, and her park. Her two homes. A chill crept up her spine. Which one did she really belong to? And how much would it hurt to see her old one, now she had given it up?

Meandering listlessly along the street, she gazed up at the leaves on the branches above her, enjoying this different view of them, and the strange juxtaposition of tall red-brick buildings with sweet smelling frangipani trees and vivid purple jacarandas.

Something slammed into her, and she cried out in shock and pain, grasping her aching arm. Turning to see what it was, she was confronted by a loud, furious man, his face red and contorted, who shouted at her to watch where she was going. Mortified, she begged his forgiveness, but he just yelled some more then strode off angrily.

Tears welled in her eyes, some from the pain, but most in reaction to the callousness of the man's response and his cruel words. He'd bumped into her, after all. She sighed. Was this what the human world was like? Her thoughts returned to the nasty boy and his father in the park. To the antagonism she'd felt from Janine. Maybe Gracie's kindness was unusual, and most people were inconsiderate and uncaring. Desperately she hoped this wasn't true.

In the meantime, she had to get used to her new senses, and her new eyesight, so she didn't bump into anyone else. As a swan, her eyes were positioned either side of her head, so she had great peripheral vision and was aware of everything happening around her, the better to keep an eye on her babies, and look out for predators. But these human eyes were so different. Their position at the front of her head narrowed her field of vision, although she had to concede that seeing ahead of her was much improved now. When someone on a two-wheeled contraption sped right at her, she quickly veered out of the way.

Maybe she'd get the hang of this human thing eventually.

What would she do with herself now though, while she waited for school to finish? She had the whole day to get through before she could return to pick Gracie up.

Sighing, she continued along the path. The sun felt good on her shoulders, and the sound of the birds overhead soothed her troubled heart. But she missed the water. Without even realising what she intended, she found herself back in her park.

Last night it had seemed scary and unfamiliar, as she'd staggered on weakened legs, dazed from her transformation and confused by the change of scale and the heavy weight of the darkness. Gazing around herself now, in the bright sunshine, she saw her home with new eyes.

Standing on top of the hill, she took in the beauty of her lake, the vivid green of the grass and the wild nature of the trees, flowers and other plants. She remembered Gracie telling her once that she and her dad were planting more trees, to help the ecosystem and all who lived in it, and she felt a surge of affection for the sweet young girl.

Slowly, cautiously, she began to descend the hill, until halfway down she started running. She laughed as the soft breeze made her long black hair dance, and the green plants became a blur out of the corner of her eye.

Before, she would occasionally leave the water to nibble on the grass and clover, but on her swan legs she was clumsy, her body heavy, and walking difficult. On these strong human legs though, she could run for miles!

Her smile faded as she reached level ground, and her steps slowed. Sunlight rippled on the surface of the lake like liquid gold, dazzling her, and its beauty moved her to tears. This was her true home. This was where she belonged. How could she have thought, even for a moment, that she could give up this place that nurtured and supported her, that *was* her? This park, this lake, this whole sacred place, it was a part of her true self, and without it she had no idea who she was.

Sinking to the ground, she dropped her head in her hands and wept.

What had she done?

Chapter 10

A not-so-gentle nudge and a loud squawk woke her, and Signet sat up abruptly. The sting of sunburn radiated across her chest and shoulders, and she sighed. She'd fallen asleep on the grass, on the shore of her lake, and now a black swamp hen was staring at her, clearly perturbed by her presence. Could it sense what she really was? Gazing into its beady little eyes, she recalled Cobie chasing this one away once, when it had tried to snatch some of the food being thrown to their brand new cygnets.

"Oh, I'm so sorry little one," she said softly, the guilt eating at her. "I guess you were hungry too, but we were both so protective of our babies that we didn't consider you. It's really tough looking after newborns, what with that eel trying to eat them and the elements sometimes being so cruel. But I'll bring you some food soon, I promise."

She smiled. "You'd love Gracie. She always makes sure everyone gets their fair share, and no one gobbles up too much. In fact, Sammy Swampie, I remember her telling you off once or twice for being a greedy guts."

The gawky black bird with the red beak regarded her coolly, and she couldn't tell if it understood her or not. She'd never really spent much time with the swamp hens of the park, preferring to stick with her own little family. Now she regretted the oversight.

The water bird squawked at her again, and she glanced down at her watch – and realised she only had fifteen minutes to get to Gracie's school.

"Oh swampie, thank you!" She leaned down slowly, wondering if it would let her stroke its soft, velvety head, but it jumped out of range of her hand with a stern honk, then hopped back to the lake's edge and plunged into the cool waters.

Laughing, she waved her hand at it, called out another thank you, then rushed along the shady tree-lined path back to the main road, then along the street to the school. She couldn't fail Gracie on her first day!

Fortunately she made good time, her ability to cope with the chaos much improved from that morning. When the final bell rang she was waiting at the gates with the other parents. Gracie smiled when she saw Signet, and raced across the playground full tilt, right at her, for a hug.

"Can we go and see the swans?" she asked hopefully, handing Signet her backpack then taking her hand.

Signet's face paled, and she froze in panic. "Um, would you like to go home for a snack first?" she asked nervously.

What impact would the absence of Gracie's swan mumma friend have on the little girl? She'd been devastated when Cobie was hurt, so she would definitely be upset to learn that his wife was now missing too. How on earth should she handle this?

Before Gracie could reply, a voice called out Signet's name across the playground. Her head whipped around in surprise, and she saw Janine hurrying towards her.

"Hi, how did Gracie go today?" she asked the teacher. "Is something wrong?"

"No... Well, nothing too serious," Janine said. "But she had an art project she should have handed in today, which she apparently couldn't do because her dad was too busy to get her the art supplies, and Ingrid of course was no help."

They both looked at Gracie, who shrugged bashfully.

"Would you be able to help her with it this afternoon Signet?" the teacher asked.

"Sure, I guess." She looked down, unable to meet Janine's eyes. "If I can." Her voice was uncertain, doubt clouding her mind and tensing her body. Perhaps she should have asked what it was before committing to it.

Ignoring her hesitation, Janine gave her a tight smile, already looking over at the line of students waiting for the bus. "Great, thanks. I'll see you both in the morning." And she rushed off to sort out another student.

"I'm sorry Signet," the little girl said quietly as they headed towards home, eyes downcast, posture forlorn.

Signet's heart ached for her. "It's okay sweetie, it's nothing to worry about."

Gracie sighed. "I really wanted to do it – it's so embarrassing being the only person who can't hand theirs in. But Daddy was working all weekend, and Ingrid was there, but she never did anything with me, just chatted to her boyfriend on the phone all day."

"It's no problem, I promise. We'll do it now," Signet said. "What do you need for it?" Anything to put off the discovery that there was no mumma swan in the park.

She was surprised when Gracie sheepishly listed all the things they needed, but there was a newsagency on their way home, which had most of the stationery supplies required, and they also had fun picking up leaves and twigs and tiny pebbles as they walked.

Her project was to make a diorama of her beloved park, with the lake cut out from blue cardboard, the trees growing from the twigs they'd collected, with fallen leaves attached, and adorable little animals Gracie cut out from a pile of the magazines they'd bought. She hadn't been able to find a black swan though, only white ones, so she asked Signet if she could draw some for her.

After the swan maiden swallowed down her panic, she picked up the black texta and did her best. She drew one of the water birds, then started another, and Gracie clapped her hands when she caught sight of the finished one.

"Oh, you've drawn the daddy swan from the park!" she exclaimed. "Are you drawing the mumma swan now?"

Gasping, Signet stared down at her. How could the little girl tell she'd been trying to draw her beloved? Didn't all swans look the same to humans? "What do you mean?" she asked nervously.

"That one looks just like Cobie, the swan husband. Will you draw his wife now?"

Signet smiled. "I'll try."

Excitement lit up Gracie's face. "I love the beautiful swan family there, they are so cute. This year they had five babies – they're called cygnets, like you! – but they've all flown away now to find their own partners and start their own families. I feel so sad for the mumma swan, being all alone now. I mean, there are lots of ducks and swamp hens on the lake, and ibises in the tree, and even a pelican, but there's just something so sweet about the swans, something so human. I'm certain that Mrs Swan knows what I'm saying when I talk to her."

Pain slammed through Signet, and she slowed her breathing, trying to control her rapid heartbeat and the tears that were pricking her eyes. "I'm sure she does. And she must be so grateful for your friendship." Her voice hitched on the last word, and Gracie gazed up at her with wide, kind eyes.

"Sometimes I feel that lonely too," the little girl admitted, then patted Signet's hand. "But I didn't mean to make you sad. I'm sorry."

Signet put down her pencil and hugged Gracie. "No need to apologise. You make me happy too."

Smiling up at her, Gracie glued Signet's self-portrait next to Cobie in the middle of the blue lake, then asked if she could draw five fluffy grey babies too.

"Then it will be perfect!"

Chapter 11

When her alarm went off the next morning, Signet barely spared it a thought. She leaped out of bed, jumped in the shower – such a strange sensation, like flying under a waterfall – then pulled on a new dress. Grabbing an apple, she headed upstairs to meet Gracie, greet Daniel on his way to work, then carefully lift the diorama so she could carry it to school for Gracie.

"I'm sorry if I made you sad last night Signet," the little girl said, just before they reached the school gates.

Squatting down carefully, so she didn't drop the delicate art project, Signet smiled at her young friend. "You have nothing to apologise for sweetie. I'm grateful that you're so kind and caring, and that we can be sad together. And I'm also glad that we cheer each other up. That's a pretty special superpower, don't you think?"

Gracie giggled and straightened one of the trees on their artwork, then took it into her arms. "You're right, yes! I'm glad we have superpowers. And thank you so much for helping me make this. It's so much better than it would have been if Ingrid had tried, not that she would have. I'm so pleased that you've replaced her."

A shadow fell across them, and Signet stood up. "Hello Janine, how are you this morning?" she asked politely. She was determined to win the woman over, no matter how long it took, and convince her of her worth.

The teacher raised her eyebrows. "I'm fine, and that diorama looks amazing Gracie, well done. Would you like a hand to take it up to the classroom?"

"Nope, I can do it all by myself," Gracie insisted, pride in her voice. Waving goodbye to Signet, she walked cautiously across the playground and disappeared inside.

"Thank you for helping her," Janine said grudgingly, as though she was surprised they'd managed to pull it off. Surprised the new nanny hadn't failed as she'd expected.

Shrugging, Signet turned back to the teacher. "I didn't need to do much at all, to be honest. I just drew a couple of swans for her. Everything else was Gracie."

Janine's smile was a little warmer this time. She obviously cared for Gracie, even if she didn't, for some reason she'd yet to reveal, like Signet. "She's a great kid, and very smart. I was devastated for her when her mum died, but she seems to be coping pretty well, considering."

"As well as can be expected I suppose."

"Her father's a wonderful man, but he works a lot, doesn't he?" the teacher pressed.

Signet nodded sadly. "It hurts him, I think, to be away from Gracie so much, but he doesn't feel like he has a choice. But he said that things will be changing soon, and he'll be able to spend more time at home."

"Good. Gracie will love that, and it will be good for both of them. No offence to you, of course."

Signet shrugged. Why would she be offended by that?

"Anyway, I'd better get inside. I'll see you this afternoon. Don't be late." And the teacher was gone, caught up in the sea of kids and the swirl of light, colour and laughter. Signet frowned. She wouldn't be late. Why had Janine said that?

Sadness settled around her. She had never felt more alone, and she walked slowly back to her apartment, head down, the cool breeze dancing through her hair barely lifting the corners of her mouth in a smile this time, and the chatter of the birds overhead scarcely registering.

Had she made a mistake giving up her feathers, and her life on the lake? Was Janine a better person to help Gracie through her grief? The teacher was a real human after all, not a fake, and she knew about human emotion. As well meaning and determined as she was, Signet was just a swan. Who was she to think she could make a difference in the little girl's life?

Once she got home, Signet dragged her feet up the stairs to her flat, and found a rolled up newspaper on the mat. Curious, she picked it up and opened the door, made a cup of green tea, then perched on the couch and read it cover to cover, fascinated by the news stories, the sports write-ups, the travel section, even the list of classifieds, which gave her an intriguing insight into humanity.

When she got up to make herself a salad for lunch, she spotted a bookshelf across the room she hadn't noticed before. Running her hands along the spines, she pulled down a title and curled up back on the couch, and was swept away into an enchanting story of magical beings and faraway realms.

From then on, each morning when she woke up, there was a new book on the shelf – a fascinating history tome, a traveller's journey, an epic fantasy, a tale of the modern world. Later, biographies and books about spirituality started to appear, and she devoured them all, spellbound, and hurting even more for Gracie and Daniel as the depth of human innovation and creativity, and emotions like empathy, loss and grief, became more apparent to her.

The kitchen intrigued her too. Part of her job was to make dinner for Gracie each night, so she spent many happy afternoons in her flat going through the items in the drawers, fridge and pantry, then poring over a cookbook she found on the shelf and experimenting with recipes. She had to be careful though, because the first time she saw a full page colour shot of a roasted chicken, and pictures of the process from plucking to baking, she felt sick. Finding out that swans used to be eaten was even more alarming.

She would stick to the vegetarian sections.

Another of the wonderful things about her new life was her improving relationship with Janine. The teacher had remained frosty for the first week, puzzling Signet with her strange hostility. Then one afternoon she'd arrived at school as normal to pick Gracie up, not knowing she had a rehearsal for the class play. Just as Signet turned to go, the teacher called her over, and they spent the time chatting together, at first about their shared affection for Gracie, but then about books they loved, tea versus coffee, and their favourite forms of exercise.

"That's easy," Signet said, beaming. "Swimming and walking in the park." Not that she'd tried swimming as a human yet, but surely the principle must be the same?

"Yoga and dancing are my favourites," Janine said. "You must be good at them too."

Signet shook her head. "I've never done yoga," she admitted. "Or danced."

The teacher stared at her, jaw dropping in shock. "What? How could you not? You would be so great at both, since you're so graceful and elegant."

Puzzled, Signet tried to recall what yoga was. It must have been mentioned in one of the books she'd read.

"You have to come to a class with me this weekend, it's just at the hall down the road. You'll love it, and you'll take to it like a duck to water, I promise," Janine said.

Signet stared at her, eyes wide with surprise. What did a class inside a hall have to do with swimming in her lake?

As it turned out, she loved the class – despite not finding out what it had to do with ducks – groaning with delight at the stretching out of her strange human body. And she enjoyed their lunch in a local cafe afterwards just as much.

"I have to apologise to you," Janine said, once their salads and green juices arrived. "I was a little… abrupt… with you when we first met. I'm just really protective of Gracie and Daniel, and you seemed, um, well, not as experienced as I'd hoped. But Gracie loves you, and you've certainly proved your dedication to her."

Taking a long sip of her juice, Signet smiled. "It's okay. I mean, I was confused at first, and a little hurt –"

Janine grimaced. "I really am sorry."

Reaching out her hand, Signet touched the other woman's arm, the way Gracie did to comfort and reassure her. "No, it's fine. I'm really glad Gracie has you as a teacher, and that you care so much about her, and her dad."

A faint blush coloured Janine's cheeks, and Signet refilled her water glass for her. She must still be hot from their workout.

"I'm not sure I should tell you this…" Janine began.

Signet looked at her in alarm. "Are you okay?"

"What? Oh, um, yes, I'm fine. It's not about me. It's just, well, before you started, Gracie was in a bad way. She was acting out, refusing to listen. One morning she got into a fight with a boy in her class, because he teased her about not having a mother."

A shiver rushed up Signet's spine, and she gazed at the teacher in horror. "I hope you explained to the boy how cruel that was, and why he should never say that again? And surely he would have been punished?"

Janine frowned. "Yes, of course, we spoke to him, but we had to discipline Gracie as well, because she started screaming at him that she hated him, and then slapped him really hard."

A memory of Gracie shouting at her first nanny, Mrs Donnelly, about how much she hated her, flashed into Signet's mind. "When was this?"

The teacher stared at her quizzically. "It doesn't really matter, does it? But I guess it was at the end of last term, so about two months ago. Just before Ingrid started looking after her, although I'm not sure *looking after her* is the right expression, because she was terribly slack. But Gracie has had a few meltdowns since then too."

Sadness crossed Janine's face, until she suddenly smiled. "Actually, the last one was just before you began. You've already made a huge difference to her."

"Really?" Signet glowed at the praise. It didn't cancel out her doubts about her transformation, or her regret at leaving Cobie, but this was the reason she'd sacrificed her old life. She'd desperately wanted to help the grieving little girl she'd come to care so deeply about, and it sounded as though she was making a difference.

"Really," Janine assured her, then turned the conversation to the book they were both reading. Her new friend had recommended it, and the next morning it had been on her bookshelf. Signet was learning so much about people and life and relationships through it, and the hopes and dreams, and desire to learn and do good, that seemed to define humanity.

Her growing friendship with Janine meant so much to her. It made her feel a little less alone, to have someone to talk to outside of her job with Gracie. Someone to laugh with, and listen to. Someone to learn about the world with, and through. Someone who chose to spend time with her, who valued her opinion, and who wanted to get to know who she was.

Which was something Signet was only just beginning to know herself, but it was a process that filled her with excitement, nerves and wild joy.

Chapter 12

"Oh no! Where has the mumma swan gone?"

Gracie's voice was panicked, and she tugged on Signet's hand, eyes desperate with worry, mouth a grimace of fear. For the past two weeks, Signet had invented a range of reasons to avoid their after-school visit to the park, from another art project to a netball game to a play date with a friend. But she was out of excuses now, and so they stood together on the shore of the lake, staring out at the ducks and swamp hens playing together, watching the murmuring ibises perched in the tree branches nearby, and both horribly aware of the absence of any swans.

"Sweetie –"

But Gracie cut her off. "I know the mumma swan was lonely after her husband had to go to hospital, but she wouldn't just fly away and leave him, would she? She wouldn't go off to a new lake to find a new home, or a new husband?"

The words were a dagger through Signet's heart, and she staggered under the weight of them. Did Cobie think she'd deserted him because she hadn't been able to find him? And if he was trapped somewhere – because the alternative didn't bear thinking about – but managed to escape, would he come back to this park looking for her, and be terrified when she wasn't here? Would he wait for her, or give up on her altogether and seek a new partner?

Her head spun, and she felt faint. Fear and regret were making her dizzy, and she sank to the ground with tears welling in her eyes. It devastated her that she had no idea where Cobie was, or if he was even still alive. What if he'd died from his injuries, and she hadn't been able to mark his passing?

Gracie collapsed down onto the grass beside Signet, and put a small hand on her shoulder. "Or would Mrs Swan be so sad she'd lost her husband that she would die of grief without him?" Her voice dropped to a whisper. "Is that what Daddy's going to do?"

Signet gasped at the question, the naked fear in Gracie's eyes piercing her defences, and she swallowed down her own worries and took the little girl's hands. "Sweetie, listen to me. Your daddy isn't going to die, and he will never leave you, I promise."

Could she promise that though? Or was she setting Gracie up for the inevitable disappointment, or worse? She sighed. Being a human was so hard. All the feelings – the anxiety, the guilt, the sadness, the grief, the confusion – were breaking her heart. She didn't know how to process them, and there were days she thought she would explode, torn apart by the emotions raging within her.

Leaning over, she hugged the little girl and stroked her hair, trying to offer what comfort she could. She would have to speak to Daniel that night and let him know the fears plaguing his daughter.

"What made you think that?" Signet pressed.

Shrugging her shoulders, Gracie mumbled something Signet couldn't hear, then gazed out over the lake. A sob shook her small body, and she swiped at her face, brushing away a tear, then visibly pulled herself together. "At least the ducks and the swamp hens are still here. Could we give them some of the peas we brought?" she asked.

"Of course!" Signet said brightly, hoping that would help soothe the young girl's distress.

Following her down to the water, she watched Gracie throw a small handful of peas to the four swamp hens who'd got there the fastest. Then, as new ones arrived, she angled a handful of the green vegies to them, making sure they all got some.

"You're so kind," Signet said. "I love that you always make sure everyone gets a little food." Abruptly she broke off. There was no way she could know that about her young charge, since this was – apparently – the first time they'd been in the park together.

But Gracie just smiled. "I wish I could introduce you to the swans. They are so beautiful. They've been coming here for the last few years to have their babies, and those bubbas are just adorable. They're so cute when they're tiny, all white-grey and fluffy and fuzzy, and they make the most adorable squeaking sounds. And as they get bigger, they slowly change. Their feathers grow darker, their necks become longer, their beaks turn red. It's the most fascinating transformation. You'd love them!"

Trying not to break down at the thought of her family, or at the irony of Gracie being so amazed by that transformation, when Signet had turned from swan to human, she nodded and forced a smile. "I'm sure I would."

For a while they chatted about the park and its inhabitants. The huge, prehistoric-looking eel that prowled through the green shallows, nibbling on sunken peas and scaring the younger water birds away. The huge white pelican, who appeared every now and then, as if by magic. The wizened old ibises, who perched in the trees telling stories. And the shy little turtles, who occasionally peeked above the surface to breathe, then darted back under if anyone was watching them.

"You remind me of the swan mumma," Gracie said, out of nowhere.

Anxiously Signet stared at her, panic bubbling up within her. How could Gracie know that? And what would happen if her secret was exposed? Would she be turned back into a bird? Or would she simply cease to exist in any form, having broken the rules so completely? "Why do you say that?" she asked shakily.

"Oh, don't be offended, it's a compliment! You're kind like her, and you listen to me. And you always seem to know when I'm feeling sad, and come over to make me feel better. Mrs Swan used to come and say hello to me too, and I would pour out my heart to her about how much I missed Mummy. I'm sure she had no idea what I was raving on about, but she looked like she was listening, and it made me feel a little bit happier to imagine that she cared about me."

Signet smiled. "I'm sure she does care about you."

The little girl's eyes lit up. "Do you really think so?"

"How could she not?"

Just then a pelican swooped down low over the lake, and Gracie squealed with excitement, leaping up to offer the visitor some peas. And when a girl came over and asked if she could feed him too, Gracie grinned, said "of course", and handed over half the remaining food.

Sighing with relief that Gracie was a bit happier now, Signet watched the two girls play, and tried to figure out what she would say to Daniel that night.

Chapter 13

The door opened just as Gracie and Signet sat down to eat, and the little girl leapt up, excited, and ran to the entranceway to hug her father.

"Daddy! You're home early. I'm so happy. We were just about to have dinner, so you can join us!"

Daniel smiled wearily. "I don't want to interrupt you both, or put Signet on the spot. She probably only made enough food for two, and I'm happy to grab some toast."

"No Daddy, there's plenty for you too. Isn't there Signet?" she asked breathlessly, eyes sparkling with joy.

"Of course." She rose and grabbed another plate, and the three of them sat and chatted about their days, as well as the school concert that was fast approaching.

It was so cosy, so normal, and Signet was happy to sit back and watch the two of them together. They got on so well, and she felt honoured to be included in this rare father-daughter moment.

It made her long for her own family though, and the ache of missing Cobie throbbed through her, bitter and sharp like a knife. Part of her was relieved when the meal ended. Standing up quickly, she started clearing the table, so she could escape to her own little haven downstairs and be miserable on her own.

"You two go into the lounge room and relax. I'll finish up here and bring you a hot milk Gracie, and would you like a chamomile tea Daniel?"

"Thank you Signet. And you should join us," he replied.

The swan maiden smiled but shook her head. "Gracie has some reading homework – she's getting so good, and she'd love to be able to read to you for once." Then she broke off, cheeks reddening. "I'm sorry, that didn't come out the way I intended."

Watching his daughter as she eagerly ran off to get her book, Daniel sighed. "No offence taken Signet, and I'd love to hear her read. It's killing me how little I'm here for her at the moment, but work has been crazy, and, well, it was a bit stressful for a while there, with just my income. But things are settling down now, and I've just been promoted, which means, ironically, that I will be able to work a little less at the office."

"Gracie will love that."

"So will I."

As she reached for his plate, Daniel laid a hand on her arm. "Thank you so much for all that you're doing for Gracie, for both of us. It's been such a weight off my mind, knowing she's in good hands, and seeing how much you care about her. Her mood and her behaviour have improved a lot since you arrived, and I'm very grateful."

"It's a pleasure, really," she said softly, glowing from the acknowledgement. "Gracie is an adorable child, and kind and sweet. She's a credit to you and…"

She broke off, flustered, and Daniel grimaced. "It's okay, you can say her name, I won't fall apart." His voice was raw, broken, and Signet blanched. She realised she didn't actually know his wife's name, which suddenly felt like a failing on her part. But Gracie just called her Mummy, and this was the longest conversation she'd ever had with Daniel.

Blinking away tears, Daniel met her worried gaze, then finally understood. "Sarah," he whispered. "Her name is Sarah. And I'm trying to be grateful for the time we did have together, rather than dwelling on it being cut so short, but it's hard. I'll always be indebted to her for the way she was with Gracie though, and I'll love her forever."

Signet wanted to reassure him, wanted to let him know she understood the pain of his loss, but Gracie bounded back in with her book then, eyes alight with anticipation, and the moment passed.

"You'll love this story Daddy, I just know it. It's mine and Signet's favourite too."

Daniel grinned at Signet, then took his daughter's hand and followed her into the lounge room. "I'm sure it will be wonderful. Is it about brave pirates, or kindly witches, or a teenage super-spy?"

Gracie's voice echoed back to Signet in the kitchen. "Don't be silly Daddy, you know my favourite stories are about swans and other animals."

Laughing quietly as she washed the dishes then put together the lunches for father and daughter for the morning, Signet was happy that at least the two would soon get to spend more time together.

As she dried the last plate and popped it back in the cupboard, Gracie burst back in and hugged Signet. "Thank you for making dinner tonight, and for having enough for Daddy. I figured you've always been cooking extra, just in case he gets home in time."

"You got me there."

Gracie giggled. "Anyway, I just came to say goodnight. But I'll see you in the morning, yes?"

"Of course! Sweet dreams sweetie."

A little while later, Daniel returned to the kitchen after tucking Gracie into bed, and sighed again. "Thank you for tonight Signet, you're amazing. Always doing everything before you're asked. Would you like a coffee, or something stronger?"

"I should be getting home," she said gently. "But, um, I thought I should share something with you." She frowned, still trying to work out the best way to say it without upsetting him, or feeling that she was betraying Gracie.

Leaning back against the bench, Daniel stared at her, suddenly serious. "Is she okay?"

"Yes, of course. Her teacher adores her, she's doing really well at school, she loves being in the play, and she has a lot of friends. But today in the park, she noticed the mother swan wasn't there, and got really upset. When I tried to comfort her, she started crying, and I finally got out of her that she's scared you're going to either fly away and leave her, and find a new family, or die of grief, which is what she decided has happened to the swan whose husband was injured."

A flash of Cobie lying unconscious in Daniel's arms threatened to undo her, and she swallowed down the tears and the lump in her throat. She wished she could thank Daniel for being so kind to her beloved, but she couldn't reveal who she was. Not that he'd believe her anyway.

Daniel had paled, and his hands clutched at the benchtop, knuckles white from the strain. "What did you tell her?" he demanded, voice tight with fear.

"I said of course you would never leave her, and you aren't going to die, but I thought maybe you could tell her in some way as well? I know why you have to work such long hours, but if you could explain it to Gracie, she might stop worrying that it's because of her. That you're trying to avoid her. Let her know that it's not her fault, and that she's not driving you away."

"Does she think that?"

Signet's mouth twisted as she considered her words, and she bit her lip. She didn't want to make the situation worse, or hurt Daniel in any way. He was a good father, he always had been. Finally she just blurted it out.

"She's concerned that you'll leave her, either intentionally or not, and she mentioned that you sometimes cry when you look at her, so she's scared that she's made you angry. Perhaps a little reassurance that you don't choose to be away from her would help, a reminder that you don't *want* to be at the office so much." She grimaced.

"Gracie is really grown up in so many ways, and is warm and empathetic, but deep down she's still just a child, trying to navigate her way through grief and the fear that she was abandoned by her mother. Not that she blames Sarah," she added quickly. "But she still feels alone at times, and lonely, and I'm not a good substitute."

"She loves you though," Daniel insisted.

"You know what I mean. Just reassure her of your love, and tell her how much you'd rather be spending time with her, and promise that you'll always be with her."

Head bowed, Daniel nodded, then forced a smile. "Thank you for having the courage to tell me that, and for caring enough about Gracie to risk upsetting me. I'll be honest, that hurt to hear, but I'm so relieved that I know now, and can help her with it."

He pulled a bottle of whiskey down from the top shelf, poured a glass, then offered one to Signet. When she shook her head, he knocked his back in a single gulp, then stared at her intently. "But what about you? How come you don't have a loved one in your life?"

Signet collapsed back against the bench, the pain of his words a visceral blow she struggled to withstand. "I do have a… partner. But he's away at the moment… for work."

Fear coursed through her veins. Was that the wrong thing to say? Would Daniel be concerned that he hadn't met this mysterious man, or even heard of him? Trying to arrest the rising panic thrumming through her veins, she took a deep breath. Did she still have a partner? Where was her beloved? Was he even alive? A wave of sadness and grief broke over her, and she blinked back the tears this unfamiliar sensation was causing. Sorrow, and longing, and an ache that burned deep within her.

Strange human emotions she was collapsing under.

Daniel poured another drink, then fought a yawn. It made Signet yawn too, and wipe away a tear. Her employer smiled at her. "Well, I hope you can be reunited soon."

"Me too," she whispered. "And on that note, I really should head off. We both need to catch up on sleep."

He laughed mirthlessly. "You're right, as usual. I'll walk you home."

"No need, I'll be down in my apartment in a flash. I'll see you tomorrow."

And she hurried out the door and down the corridor and away before he could hug her, certain that any sympathy would be her undoing. She was emotionally drained from the day, and couldn't wait to collapse into bed and drift off into dreams.

Dreams of sun-drenched summer lakes, and gliding across the glittering surface with her beloved. Of curling up with him in winter, and sharing nesting duties, and looking after their cygnets together.

But sleep eluded her, and she tossed and turned all night, scared she'd said or done something wrong. Had she made things worse for Gracie by confiding her secrets to her father? She was just a swan after all. What did she know about the lives and loves and losses of humans?

Chapter 14

"Will you read me a story please Signet?" Gracie asked a few nights later, as she pulled her pyjamas on and climbed into bed.

"Um, sure, what would you like to hear?"

Settling back against the pillows, the little girl pointed to her bookshelf. "Something from the faery tale book."

Signet raised her eyebrows. What was a faery tale? Did humans know stories about the tiny beings that buzzed around the park coaxing the flowers to bloom, and the water sprites they shared the lake with? As she lifted the book down, she marvelled at the beautiful cover and its depiction of the beings she knew so well. It seemed someone human had seen them too.

"This one? *Thirty Tales of Magic?*" she asked. "Which one should I read for you?"

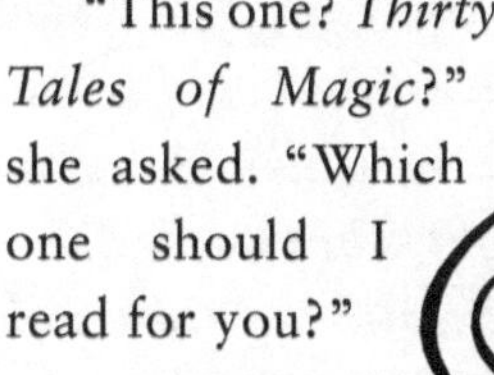

Gracie shrugged. "You choose. I love them all. Maybe just open to a page at random, and read me that one. That's how Mummy used to pick them." Her voice shook on the last few words, but she smiled bravely at Signet. "Thank you for spending so much time with me. I still miss her so much, but you make me feel safe and happy."

This girl seemed to have superpowers – she could bring Signet to tears without much effort at all. Trying to pull herself together, the swan maiden opened the book to a third of the way in, then smiled at Gracie.

"This one is called *The Selkie*, is that all right?"

Gracie nodded and snuggled into the warm cocoon of her bed. "That's a good one. It's sad though, is that okay?"

Signet smiled. "If it's okay with you?"

The little girl nodded, so Signet sank down onto the edge of her bed, and began to read.

Once upon a time, there were seven beautiful seal sisters. They loved each other dearly, and lived a happy, peaceful life. They loved swimming in the crystal clear ocean together, playing in the swell with passing dolphins, heading off on adventures to explore nearby islands, and occasionally going ashore on moonlit nights so they could dance together on the golden sand.

For once a month, as the sun set in a blaze of colour in the west and the full moon rose in the east, the seven sisters would slip out of their sealskins, stash them behind a rock, and then, transformed into human women, give themselves over to the magic of the night. They adored the feel of the cool air on their skin, the sensation of the wind rippling through their long wavy hair, the crispness of the sand beneath their human feet, the beauty of the gilded light as it drenched them in moonbeams, and the sense of freedom they felt as they swayed to the music of the crashing waves and the cawing of sea birds.

Shocked, Signet gazed at the illustration on the page, her eyes widening as she saw the beautiful women stepping out of their skins and tiptoeing onto the sand on human legs, before being swept up in the dance.

Did they stagger on the same unsteady legs she had walked on when she shed her cloak of black feathers and took human form? Is that what they were doing too? Had it happened before? Were all creatures able to perform this magic?

She looked back down at the words on the page, mind whirring with possibility, and kept reading.

One night, as the full moon sank towards the horizon and the first signs of dawn's approach coloured the eastern sky, the sisters hurried over to the rock and slipped their sealskins back on, then dove elegantly into the water. But the youngest sister was horrified to discover that her skin was missing.

Panic gripped her. Where had it gone? What would she do, trapped here on the land? She'd heard tales from her grandmother, warnings that they must always be back in the ocean by the time the sun rose, lest they be stuck forever in the inbetween, cursed to remain human, and slowly sicken and die from lack of water.

Her heartwrenching sobs alerted her siblings, and the six sleek seals swam back to the shallows.

"What is wrong dear sister? Why haven't you joined us yet? Hurry, the sun will soon rise."

Her cries grew louder, and more human, and they struggled to understand her words.

"Help me, please! My sealskin has gone, and here I am stuck," she wailed.

Signet wanted to sob too, but she tried to keep her emotions under control. "It is sad," she whispered.

Gracie was staring at her with big round eyes. "Keep going," she said, voice high with emotion. "It gets worse."

Worse? Should she be reading this to the little girl? Gracie had already suffered enough heartbreak. Did she need to hear about more?

"I still love it though," the little girl said. "And it's all okay in the end. Keep reading!" she urged her.

Reluctantly Signet turned the page and continued.

The seal maiden's oldest sister swam as close as she dared, and her sleek seal head bobbed above the waves. "Dear sister, we will return to you tonight," she called. "Try to find shelter, or shade. A cave perhaps, or even a tree. Don't let the sun dehydrate you."

And she did an elegant somersault and was gone.

The youngest sister tried to calm her racing heart and focus. Yes, she needed shelter. But before she could decide which direction to go in, she heard footsteps behind her, and spun around in terror, trying to cover her naked body with her long dark hair.

It was a man, one of the fishermen who resided on these lonely islands, who she had long seen but never spoken to, never revealed herself to. She trembled with fear.

"Don't be afraid, beautiful maiden. I have your skin," he said.

"Oh, how wonderful. Please, may I have it back? I need to return to the water before I sicken."

The man's expression hardened, and a sly smile twisted his lips upwards.

"I don't think so, seal lady. I have your skin, and thus I have your life. And so you will be my wife."

The seal sister opened her mouth to scream, but no sound came out. Her vocal cords were frozen in shock. The man grabbed her roughly by the arm, and she twisted herself in all directions, trying to escape. But he was too strong. He dragged her up the beach and along the path to a small, tumbledown cottage.

"This is where you will live now. And you will cook for me, and clean, and be my wife."

She cried and she begged, to no avail. She explained that she had a husband already, and a home beneath the waves, but the man just laughed. And that very day he slid an old, mouldering, sack-like white gown over her head and marched her down to the local church. There they were married by the priest, who ignored her tears and her pleas, happy just to be paid for the service, no questions asked.

Heart hammering in her chest, Signet paused again. This story was so haunting, and so tragic. She wanted to stop reading, wanted to scream at the man, hurt him even. She wanted to cry her eyes out for the poor little seal sister, trapped against her will in a realm she was not part of, where she couldn't live or thrive.

Some days the thought of being human devastated Signet, and she longed for her old home on the lake. But at least she'd had a choice. It was her decision to transform, to sacrifice her past and leave her old life, so that she could help Gracie. The young seal sister had no say in the matter though. She was a prisoner, ripped away from her family and loved ones in the cruellest way, and trapped in a place she didn't want to be.

"Are you okay Signet?" Gracie asked in a small voice. "We don't have to keep going with this one. We can read the one about the princess in an enchanted sleep, or about the young boy who challenges a giant and wins."

Signet smiled. "I'm okay, I just feel so sad for the poor seal maiden. To be kidnapped like that –"

"Faery tales always have an underlying tragedy to them," Gracie said softly. "But there is hope in them too, and the chance to grow, or so Mummy always said. And I promise there's a happy ending for the seal sister."

"Okay then, let's do this."

Chapter 15

For the next seven years, the seal sister's life was spent in the cottage, cooking and cleaning and submitting to her so-called husband's will – and, whenever he was out fishing, searching desperately for her sealskin.

During the first year, she would slip outside at midnight every full moon, and rush on silent feet down to the beach to dance with her sisters. They would hug her and braid her hair with seaweed, and tell her what was happening beneath the waves, then wipe her tears and console her as the first rays of dawn's light meant they had to leave her.

On the sixth full moon, when she was starting to wonder if she could bear to see them any more, her sisters told her they had found a sea witch who would concoct a potion to help her escape the human world

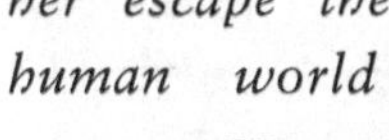

and change back to her seal self. She spent the following days wandering the seashore humming happily, dreaming of her return to her beloved watery realm, and being reunited with her seal husband.

But on their next visit her sisters arrived dejected, with the dreadful news that the witch's spell had failed. They all put on a brave face, and promised that they would still find a way to bring her home, but each month their hopes sank lower as no solution presented itself.

The partings with her seal sisters became sadder each time, and on the thirteenth full moon since her capture, when her jailer-husband followed her down to the beach and threatened to burn the sealskins of all of her sisters, she reluctantly whispered to them that they must not return to her.

It broke her heart to send them away, but she couldn't risk their freedom. She would have to resign herself to this miserable human life, and find a way to continue without the lunar meetings that had sustained her until now.

Seeing her sorrow, her fisherman captor started treating her with a little more kindness, and they reached an uneasy truce. A year later she gave birth to their first son, a year later they had another, and a year after that, a daughter was born. Her children were the only thing that kept her going and made her stolen life almost bearable, and she was a wonderful mother to them. She especially loved her little girl, who followed her adoringly all day, and refused to leave her mother's side, even when her brothers went out fishing with their father.

Most days the seal sister got up before her family woke and silently slipped outside, so she could wander the shore alone, letting the sound of the waves soothe her bitterness, and hoping desperately for a glimpse of the bobbing heads of her long-lost siblings and husband beyond the breakers.

But the longer she stayed on dry land, the less connected she felt to her old life, her old self, her old home, and the less able to distinguish the features of one sister from another or comprehend what they were trying to tell her. They would stare up at her with their huge sad eyes, then slowly swim away.

Signet inhaled sharply, and stared at Gracie in consternation. Would she start to forget her old life, her old family, her old self, the longer she stayed here in the human world? And what if Cobie returned to the park, but she didn't recognise him?

"Keep going! We're getting to the best part," Gracie said, eyes shining with hope and excitement.

Reluctantly Signet kept reading.

"Are you sick Mama?" her daughter asked, one long summer day when the seal sister couldn't get out of bed. The heat affected her badly, and she craved the ocean even more at this time of year. Although she had no mirror, she knew her skin was drying out, lines were ravaging her face, and she was worryingly thin. She needed the water. She needed to swim in the ocean. She needed her freedom.

She needed her sealskin.

Tenderly she smiled at her daughter. "I'm sorry sweetheart. I've lost my favourite dress, and without it I get so tired, and feel so sick." She could feel death hovering. She knew she would die within the week, and it broke her heart that she would leave her children alone. She was even more devastated that she would never get to say goodbye to her seal husband, or dance with her seal sisters one more time.

Tears welled in Signet's eyes, and Gracie patted her hand. "That's not fair is it, to have been taken away from her family? She probably had seal babies too, and they would be missing their mummy. Not to mention her husband! It's a bit like the swans in our lake. I still feel so sad for the one whose husband was hurt by that boy. Do you think they'll ever find each other again?"

Signet's heart swelled with love for this kind young girl. She'd lost so much herself, yet she still cared about others. "I hope they will," she whispered.

"Me too," Gracie said fiercely. Then her voice softened, became tentative. "Do you think Daddy will ever find another wife, or is he like a swan, with only one true love for his whole life?"

"Oh sweetie, I hope he will. He definitely deserves to find love again." Everyone did. "Do you want another Mummy?" she asked cautiously.

The little girl shrugged. "I have Daddy, and you, so I'm okay. I just feel sad for Daddy."

Signet reached down and stroked her cheek. "You are a remarkable child Gracie. I hope you never lose your kind heart."

Giggling, Gracie put a hand to her chest. "I could never lose that silly, it's stuck inside me! How could it fall out?"

"Silly me," Signet agreed, momentarily cheered by the lightened mood.

"Keep reading, this is the good bit!" Gracie said.

Signet was beginning to doubt that any good could come of this story, but she dutifully returned to it.

"Which dress?" her daughter asked.

A wild flicker of hope flared in the seal sister's chest, then was just as quickly extinguished, leaving her feeling more defeated than ever. "My silver one. But it's long gone. I haven't had it for years, haven't seen it..."

Her daughter tugged on her hand. "You mean the one in the loft above Father's boat?"

The seal sister's breath caught. Surely it hadn't been here, so close, all along? She'd searched everywhere for it, day after day after day. "You've seen it?"

Her daughter smiled. "Yes, one day when the boys were sick and I helped Father with the fish. I can show you where it is."

Hardly daring to breathe, let alone hope, she dragged herself out of bed and followed her daughter on shaking legs. When the small child scurried up the ladder to the loft, she could only stare in wonder, too weak to climb after her. But soon her daughter re-emerged with a large silver-grey bundle in her arms, face wreathed in smiles, and looking very proud of herself.

"This one Mama?"

Dizzy with relief and joy, the seal sister sank to the floor. Her daughter ran to her in a panic, dropping the bundle into her lap. "What's wrong? Are you okay?"

Her mother gazed up at her through tear-stained eyes. "Oh my darling, yes. I've never been better."

Yet now that she had her sealskin – her self – in her arms, her heart was breaking in two. How could she leave her beloved daughter, and her sons? She'd felt only half alive all these years because she'd yearned for her seal husband and their family. Would she spend the rest of her life devastated by the loss of these precious children? How could she make such a terrible choice?

"Put it on Mama, show me. It's so beautiful." Her daughter was stroking the sleek "fabric" of the garment, a sense of peace and contentment on her face. And the seal sister realised with a flash that her children were seal people too, at least half. Did her daughter know, on some subconscious level, what this "dress" represented?

And did she have the strength to put it on and leave this house, this world, these children?

"Don't be sad." Her daughter was crouched by her side, eyes burning with a strange, wild intensity. "You have to get better Mama, otherwise you'll die, and then no one will have you."

Shocked, the seal sister stared at the girl, and saw for the first time the sea swimming in her deep blue eyes. Saw the sleek seal nature of her smooth dark hair. She stood up, sealskin under her arm, and reached for her mother's hand. "Come, we'll go together."

The stress of her choice and the depths of her illness were making the seal sister's head spin, but she took her daughter's small hand in hers and followed her down to the beach. She was staggering by the time they reached the shoreline, but her child never loosened the grip on her fingers, propelling her forward when she would have stumbled and fallen on the golden sand.

When the comforting chill of the grey ocean swirled around her toes, she lifted her face to the horizon, and saw a sleek silver head out past the shallows, watching her intently. Falling to her knees in the cold water, she cried out, a cry of deep pain and anguish. Her beautiful daughter had found her freedom for her – but she would be the one to pay the heaviest price. And how angry would her father be with her, that she had released her mother from his awful enslavement? Could she really leave her alone to suffer his cruel wrath?

"Don't cry Mama," her daughter said. She was untying the strap around the bundle she still cradled in her arms, her movements slow and deliberate.

"But my darling child, how can I leave you?" the seal sister sobbed.

The girl smiled. "But you're not leaving me, silly, I'm coming with you."

And she reached within the sealskin and drew out a small pair of gloves made from the same material.

"What –?" her mother asked, breath held, hardly able to believe her eyes.

"A gift from my aunty," the daughter said, and grinned.

After pressing the large skin into her mother's arms, she pulled the gloves on, and the seal sister watched in amazement and awe as the sleek silver-grey skin of the gloves moulded around her hands then slowly spread up her arms and over her shoulders.

Her daughter was transforming from human to seal right before her eyes, and she laughed with delight, sending a prayer of gratitude to whichever of her sisters had made this possible.

Eagerly stepping into her own skin, she took her daughter's sleek grey hand and dove into the ocean, overjoyed when her seal husband swam over to them, embraced them both, then led them down under the waves, to the watery realm where they belonged.

Every year on her sons' birthdays, the seal sister rose to the ocean surface to watch them as they played on the beach, and was relieved beyond measure to see that they at least were thriving with their father.

When they turned thirteen, they would be offered the option to join her, and she would accept whatever choice they made. For knowing where you truly belong, and who with, is the greatest secret of all. And the freedom to be your true self is just as important, just as essential to life, as loving and being loved.

Gracie clapped her hands together in delight. "Isn't that beautiful! She had her human daughter *and* her seal family, and she was still connected with her sons as well. So in the end, she had everyone and every thing she'd ever loved."

Signet was astounded, by the story and by the young girl before her. Laughing, she threw her arms around Gracie and embraced her.

Maybe there was hope for her yet.

Chapter 16

"Can I come home with you today?" Gracie asked as they crossed the school playground together one afternoon.

Signet looked down at her young charge and smiled. "Sure. Will your dad mind though?"

The little girl laughed mirthlessly. "He won't even know, because he'll still be at work, as usual. But don't worry, he suggested it, because they were painting in our place this morning, where the water leaked, and the caretaker said we should stay out as long as possible to air it out."

"I just hope you won't be bored," Signet said cautiously. "I don't have any toys or games or anything."

Gracie giggled. "I didn't think you'd have toys, silly! But you could show me

how to make those yummy gingerbread bikkies you brought us last week, right?"

Decision made, they wandered home through the late afternoon sunshine, chatting about Gracie's classes, her school friend who had the measles, and the upcoming play. Contentment settled over Signet. She loved spending time with Gracie, and as she listened to her recounting her day, she could almost imagine she was the little girl's mother. Could almost forget she'd once had a husband and a family of her own.

"Signet, thank you for speaking to Daddy."

"Hmm?" They'd made it upstairs, and got the tray of gingerbreads in the oven, so now Signet had one eye on the biscuits and the other on the mixing bowl Gracie was stirring so casually. Visions of cake batter all over the floor were distracting her from their conversation.

"We had a big talk last night, and he explained why he has to work so much, and said you told him I was worried about his long hours."

Suddenly the little girl had her complete attention, and she gulped nervously. "Was that okay?"

"Yes, of course! Because he said your conversation encouraged him to speak to his boss, and soon he'll be able to leave early enough to pick me up from school, and spend heaps more time with me. Isn't that great!"

"It's wonderful." Signet tried to smile, tried to hide her sigh. It *was* wonderful, yet she felt the shock of it like a body blow. What would that mean for her? Would she be out of a job when Daniel no longer needed her to pick up the slack in caring for Gracie? How would she survive in the human world without her purpose for being here, and the wage that kept her in food and paid her bills?

Beaming, Gracie stuck her finger in the cake batter and tasted it, then pronounced it ready to bake. "While you pour it in the tin and stick it in the oven, can I use your bathroom please?" she asked.

"Of course, just through there. And it won't take long to cook, so we'll have it cooled and iced and ready for dessert tonight."

When Gracie left the kitchen, Signet popped the cake in the oven then started washing up, surprised by the huge mess they'd made, but glad for the distraction from her thoughts that cleaning provided. Maybe Daniel would recommend her to one of the other parents at Gracie's school, or perhaps she could work in the kitchen of a cafe, washing dishes while she proved her cooking skills. There were a few vegetarian restaurants in the area, and they often had Help Wanted flyers pinned to their noticeboards.

A gasp from the other room brought her back to the present, and Signet spun around to see Gracie emerge from her bedroom with her black-feathered cloak held reverently in her arms.

"It's so beautiful," the little girl cried, fingers gently stroking it. "And it's perfect!"

Signet stared at her, alarmed. How had she found it? What was she doing with it? And why could she feel every stroke of Gracie's hand on her own body, as she touched the cloak? Was it really still a part of her, like the selkie's sealskin from that story? And would she always remain connected to it, even though she'd made the decision to give up her swan life?

She shivered. Was it as real as her? As alive as her? And if Cobie did return, would he be able to sense her – or would he only sense the feathers? What if it was ever lost?

Wait! What was it perfect for?

A chill crawled up Signet's spine and left her shaking, and she stared nervously at Gracie, who was jumping up and down, radiant with excitement.

"Um, Signet, could I pretty please borrow this for the school play? I promise I'll look after it, and guard it with my life. It's just so perfect, because I'm playing a black swan, and until now all Miss Henwood has come up with is a black dress with a few feathers around the neckline."

Waves of shock rolled over Signet. Gracie was playing her in the school play, a sweet, if somewhat unsettling, thought. But she wanted to wear her actual feather cloak, and to take this secret part of her out of her home and let other people see it. Just thinking about it made her heart pound, her body weak, and her whole self feel exposed.

Through her agitation, she finally noticed the trembling pout on Gracie's face, and the disappointment in her eyes. And for better or worse, Signet couldn't bear to disappoint the little girl. Gulping down her anxiety, she spoke quickly, before she could change her mind.

"Of course you can wear it. But you must be very careful with it, okay? It was... a gift from my husband, and there's no way I can replace it if it's damaged."

Nodding gravely, Gracie gave her an earnest smile. "You can trust me with it Signet, I promise. I know how important it is to you. But it will help me, I know it. I'm so scared about being in the play, yet this will give me confidence."

"I do trust you sweetie. How about I take it up to the school for you though, since it's so heavy?"

Shoulders slumping, Gracie reluctantly nodded, and set the cloak down on the couch, but she kept stealing glances at it the whole time she was in the flat.

A week later was parent-teacher night, and Daniel came home from it smiling widely, congratulating Gracie on her excellent work that term, and thanking Signet for all her help and encouragement, scholarly and emotional, which Janine had made a point of mentioning.

"Your teacher is a lovely woman Gracie," he said, and Signet watched, intrigued, as his cheeks reddened a little. "I hope you appreciate her."

"I do Daddy. And I like her much better than last year's mean one. Miss Henwood is nice, like Mummy, and Signet."

Daniel smiled at Signet over his daughter's head, and she basked in the warmth of the compliments. This was why she'd given up her life on the lake, given up her very self, so she was relieved that she was making a difference, and her sacrifice hadn't been wasted.

The following night was the school concert, and Daniel invited Signet to go with him so they could both cheer Gracie on. It was strange for her to sit in the darkened hall, surrounded by hundreds of parents clutching cameras and eager for a glimpse of their child, bragging to their neighbour about sporting achievements, test results and art prizes, and the roles their offspring were playing that night.

After a cute song from the first graders, the curtain opened and the lights went up, and Signet froze. Gracie was standing in the centre of the stage, the black-feathered cloak tied at the neck and swirling out around her, swamping her small frame. It could have looked ridiculous, a child playing dress-ups, but it didn't. She looked calm, confident, regal.

As Signet watched, Gracie seemed to grow taller, or the feather cloak got smaller, both shifting so that now they seemed the perfect size, as though they had been made for each other. As though they were *part* of each other.

"No!" she whispered, horrified. Her hands shook and her head swam, and she wrapped her arms around herself protectively. Gracie couldn't be transforming into a swan, like the little girl in the Selkie story had changed into a seal, could she? Not under these bright spotlights, in front of all these people, as Signet helplessly watched.

Not in real life.

Could the magic work both ways? Ibis Man had said she couldn't change back, that she'd used up all the power when she chose to give up her swan self to become human. But could someone else tap in to it? Could *Gracie* go back?

Her heart raced, and her skin turned clammy with fear and sweat. When she felt a hand on her arm, she jumped, and looked to her right in panic.

Daniel was smiling at her. "Doesn't she look wonderful? Thank you so much for making Gracie's costume for her, it's perfect. I was worried she wouldn't be able to find the courage to go onstage, but you've given her that. It's an amazing gift." And he calmly snapped another photo.

Costume. Courage.

Signet gazed back at the stage, eyes fixed anxiously on Gracie, but now she did just look like a girl in a fancy dress costume. Not a girl changing into a swan.

Exhaling, she tried to relax, to become swept up in the play. Her young charge was moving around the stage with confidence and great poise, her voice projecting to every corner of the hall. She was blossoming before their eyes, transforming from a shy, quiet little girl into a powerful, assured performer, but that was all. And that was enough.

That was its own enchantment.

Relieved, Signet settled back in her seat, and finally allowed herself to relax. For a moment she watched Daniel's face as he watched his daughter. There was awe, and sadness, and great love, and it warmed her heart to see a father so dedicated and devoted to his child. Just like Cobie.

A sweet melody drew her attention back to the stage, and as Gracie spun around, the blue-black sheen of her feathers rippled under the lights. Signet ached for all she had left behind, and the dull throb of yearning pulsed through her. Her life here was full, and good, but she missed the freedom of the lake and the magic of the great outdoors, of the sky stretching so far above her it was as though the world went on forever.

And she missed her beloved so much. They should have been fixing their nest right now, planning how to best share the shifts of sitting on their eggs, and preparing to welcome their new babies. Her mothering instincts were mostly fulfilled by her time with Gracie, but it wasn't quite the same as paddling around the lake with her fluffy little cygnets on her back, watching Cobie play with them, and keeping them safe from the park's sinister eel.

Even more than that, she wondered who she was now. The words of the Selkie story haunted her. Reading the end, about the importance of being your true self, and how the freedom to be that is as essential as loving and being loved, had been like a mortal body blow, shattering every belief she held. The seal sister had been only half alive as a human, her real self suppressed, as trapped emotionally as she was physically. And she'd sickened and almost died because she was so cruelly kept from her home and her family.

It scared Signet. Had *she* given up her true self when she transformed? Or was she still as much who she'd always been now, as a human, as when she was a swan? She didn't feel any different, and in some ways she felt even more herself, but how would she know? Could she just not see it, not realise that she was as trapped as the seal sister?

Swallowing down the tears starting to thicken in her throat, she glanced at Daniel. She'd felt sorry for him because he was alone, still grieving his wife, and focused only on work and his daughter, but she was the same, just as alone. Just as devastated. And she didn't even know if she was capable of human love. Here she was worrying about her true self, when she'd lost her true love.

But hopefully it was different for her because she'd *chosen* to give up her swan self in order to help Gracie, rather than being abducted and forced to change. As the curtain fell and the room broke out in wild applause, she prayed that was true.

When the last performance was over, everyone gathered backstage, the children giggling as they drank lemonade and tried to calm down after the adrenaline rush of being on stage. Daniel was chatting to some of the parents he knew but hadn't seen for some time, and Signet leaned against a wall, sipping a cup of tea and smiling at Gracie's exuberance, content just to watch the colourful swirl of humanity as it seethed and swelled around her.

She'd been reading a romance novel that day, and she was still puzzling over the behaviour of the two main characters. They clearly liked each other, but neither of them would say anything – in fact they tried to avoid each other – so she was thoroughly confused. Unfortunately the adults in the room tonight were already coupled, so they shed no light on it for her.

A tap on her shoulder jolted her back, and she turned to see Janine, holding two cupcakes, a huge smile on her face. Signet took one of the cakes, then hugged her friend. "Congratulations on the play, it went so well," she said. "And Gracie was amazing. You did such a good job, because I know how nervous she was about being on stage."

Janine shook her head. "Thanks, but you deserve the credit, not me. She was still scared tonight, until she slipped on the costume you made her. She said she felt you with her, and would call on your courage to make it through."

Grinning with pleasure, Signet glanced over at Gracie, who smiled at her and gave her a thumbs up. She started to say something to Janine, then realised her friend's eyes, and all her attention, were on Daniel, and she had a goofy smile on her face. *Oh.*

She thought back to some of the teacher's previous comments about him, and her blushes and stammering. Did her friend *like* Daniel? Then she remembered the way Daniel had reddened last night when he said how wonderful Janine was, and she laughed, delighted.

"He really is a lovely man, isn't he?" she said softly.

Janine turned back to her, and blushed again. "He is. And it was great to be able to talk to him last night about Gracie, and share what a great kid she is."

"He loved talking to you too," Signet said, eyebrows raised, and a knowing look on her face.

The teacher's eyes widened. "What do you mean?"

"I can tell how much you like him."

Blinking rapidly, Janine gasped and took a step back, putting some distance between them. "What? I don't know what you're talking about. How could you think that? I'd never dream of coming between the two of you."

Signet stared at her, confused. Coming between her and Daniel? What did that mean? Then a scene from the novel she was reading flashed into her head, and understanding dawned. "Oh, no, it's not like that. I'm not involved with Daniel romantically, if that's what you're wondering." She touched the other woman's arm, trying to soothe and reassure her. "I'm only Gracie's nanny, nothing more."

Her friend's cheeks turned bright red, but she saw a spark of hope ignite in her eyes.

"He really appreciates all you do for Gracie, he said so last night," Signet continued boldly. "And I think he likes you too."

"What?" Janine shrieked.

But Signet couldn't tell her about Daniel's matching blushes, because he was walking towards them, holding Gracie's hand, and Janine was trying to compose herself while Signet tried to hide her amusement.

"Good evening Miss Henwood," Daniel began. "It was a wonderful performance tonight, and I wanted to thank you for encouraging Gracie's thespian side."

Janine blushed, and tried to shrug off the compliment. "Thank you for coming, and, um, for last night. Well, talking about Gracie last night I mean…"

For a moment they stared at each other, then they both looked away, and spoke at the same time.

"I was wondering if –"

"Could I get you a –"

"Oh, you first…"

"No, you…"

Signet grinned. The novel she'd been reading was starting to make sense. All the furtive glances and blushes, all the nervous greetings and awkwardness.

"Gracie, let's go and grab some food, and get your dad a cup of tea," Signet said. She looked at her friend. "Would you like one too Janine?"

The teacher nodded absently, and Signet took Gracie's hand and wandered over to the food table with her. Gratified that all the cupcakes she'd baked for the occasion were already gone, she picked up a swan-shaped cookie covered in black icing, and handed one to Gracie too.

"You were so wonderful tonight sweetie. Did you enjoy being on stage?"

Gracie beamed at her. "It was so much fun! And it was so wonderful to look out and see you and Daddy sitting there together, watching. If Mummy couldn't be here, I'm glad it was you."

"I'm sorry she couldn't be."

"Me too." Gracie bit into a cookie, then changed the subject. "Miss Henwood made these ones, to match the play. Aren't they yummy. Not as delicious as your cupcakes, obviously, but not too bad."

Signet laughed.

"Do you think she would make a good mummy one day?" Gracie asked.

Signet almost choked on the biscuit. "What?"

"Well, for a while I was hoping that you would be my mummy, and come and live with us, but you said the other day that you already have a husband, so I'm guessing that means you can't marry Daddy, right?"

"That's right, I do have a husband sweetie, he's just... away... at the moment." Her voice hitched, the pain sneaking up on her, flooding her mind and body with bitter sorrow. Yet Gracie's story of the seal sister finally being reunited with her seal husband had given her a glimmer of hope that she would some day, some way, be able to return to hers too. She wasn't sure how, but she was determined to figure it out.

"But yes, I think Miss Henwood might make you and your father very happy one day."

Chapter 17

"Are you sure it's okay to look after her again today?" Daniel asked, anguish and regret in his voice. "You deserve to have one day a week off."

Leaning forward to touch his arm reassuringly, as she'd seen others do, Signet smiled. "Of course, it's fine. I had no plans today, and Gracie has been wanting to go to the zoo for weeks. She's made it sound pretty awesome, so I'll probably have just as much fun as she does, and today is the perfect day for it. We'll both enjoy the ferry ride across the harbour too, so please don't worry. She understands that you have to work."

"I really hope so." Opening his briefcase, Daniel took out his wallet and gave Signet some money. "For the tickets, and whatever else you might need. I wish I could go with you both," he said wistfully. "But once I land this deal, work will calm down, and I'll be able to spend more time with Gracie, I promise... Ah, speak of the devil!" He laughed as his daughter raced into the kitchen, and scooped her up for a hug.

"Can we go to the zoo today Daddy, can we, can we?"

Signet smiled. "We can indeed. Do you have your hat?"

"Of course, silly." She looked at her dad. "Can you come with us?" she asked, although there was less hope in her voice this time, and when he reluctantly said no, she only shrugged and turned away. She didn't try to change his mind, because she recognised it was a lost cause.

Signet's heart hurt for them both. She knew how much Daniel would prefer to spend the day with his daughter, but also how pressured he was at the office, and as a single-income family. But it was hard to explain that to a disappointed seven-year-old.

Swallowing down his own sadness, Daniel kissed Gracie goodbye and quickly left for work, and Signet smiled brightly, determined to help Gracie have a wonderful day. Packing a straw basket with sunscreen, water and snacks, she led her downstairs and out to the bus stop. The little girl cheered up when the bus started moving, pointing out the flowers along their route.

"Mummy loved those purple ones, the jacarandas," she told Signet. "The trees are all green leaves for a while, then they're suddenly covered in purple blooms, then when the petals fall it's like a pretty purple carpet on the ground."

"They're gorgeous."

"And Mummy loved those frangipanis too, the creamy flowers that smell so sweet. She had a frangipani perfume, so I always think of her when I see them."

Gracie sighed and stared out the window, quiet for a while, and Signet put an arm around her, trying to comfort her. But when they got to the harbour and climbed off the bus, the little girl saw some seagulls and smiled, then ran straight towards them. "Hello birdies!" she cried happily. "Don't fly away, I won't hurt you."

Sagging against a pylon with relief, Signet whispered a prayer of thanks to the gulls. Sunshine, flowers and birds had cheered Gracie up, and when they climbed aboard the ferry, she was just as enthralled by the sparkling water and the cool breeze on her face.

And so was Signet.

"Come up here," Gracie called out to her, so the swan maiden scrambled over the railing and joined the little girl at the very front of the boat. Excitement pulsed through her. It felt like she was flying over the lake in the park, the dazzling surface of the harbour glistening in the sunshine, and the air blowing her hair back as though it was feathers. Swallowing over the lump in her throat, she opened her arms wide, closed her eyes, and imagined that she was back there, wings touching Cobie's as they soared through the bright blue sky together.

"It's like we're birds, isn't it?" Gracie exclaimed, her laughter floating out behind them like ribbons in the wind.

By the time they'd climbed the hill to the zoo their legs were aching, and as they walked through the turnstile at the entrance, Signet was overwhelmed by the cacophony of sounds, the vivid blue-skied haze of heat, and the awful crush of people pushing against her. Her head swam, and she stumbled on the steps – and would have fallen if Gracie hadn't grabbed her hand and steadied her.

Mumbling an apology, she took a deep breath, and meekly followed in the young girl's wake as she strode along the paths to visit her favourite animals. It was beautiful to watch her chatting with the creatures, and Signet's mind drifted back to her life on the lake, when Gracie had spent so much time talking to her and Cobie, and getting to know their children.

She missed it. The park, the lake, her family, her beloved. Missed the peaceful days of gliding across the water with Cobie. The shared adventures of guarding the nest then caring for their babies. The fun they'd had as their cygnets grew up, then the emotional charge of teaching them to fly so they could eventually take off on their own journeys, find their own partners and create their own happy families.

Sipping water and walking slowly as she tried to shake off the dizziness, Signet was vaguely aware that they'd reached the Australian animals section. She smiled as Gracie peered up at the koalas in their trees and clicked her tongue at the kangaroos nibbling on the grass, while still dreaming of her own life back in her beautiful park.

But a cry from Gracie instantly got her attention.

"Signet, look!"

Rushing over, her heart skipped a beat when she saw what Gracie was pointing at. It was Cobie, paddling across the waters of the wetland birds area.

Her beloved, healed and whole, and very much alive.

She could barely catch her breath, sucking in air in great gulps. He was okay.

Her legs wobbled and her knees buckled, the relief overwhelming. Sinking to the grass in wonder, she clung to Gracie's hand, then rubbed her eyes, suddenly scared she'd imagined it.

But no. When she opened them again, he was still there.

"Oh my love," she whispered, and slowly began to weep.

One of the animal carers approached them. "What is it?" she asked, amused by their unusual response to the ordinary black swan they were staring at so intently.

"That's our friend," Gracie said, pointing at Cobie.

"He's a lovely creature."

"No, he's not a creature, he's our friend," Gracie insisted. "Signet's husband."

Both women stared at her, mouths open in shock.

"What?" Signet stuttered.

Gracie looked at her with a cheeky smile. "I was so sad when you were left on your own, because I could tell how much you missed your husband when he got hurt and was taken away by the wildlife person, and how distressed you were that you never knew if you'd see him again. But then you came to help me because I missed my mummy so badly, and I hoped I could help you too."

The zoo worker was staring at them both as if they were crazy, but Signet didn't care. She was enthralled. Desperately she hung on every one of Gracie's words, astounded that the young girl had recognised Cobie, who surely looked like any other black swan to a human. Then again, she'd been able to identify all five of their cygnets.

But how on earth had she known who *she* really was? *What* she really was? Or was it just a figure of speech, her imagination on overdrive? That made more sense, surely.

Gracie seemed oblivious to her confusion, far more concerned with the fact that they'd found Cobie.

They'd found Cobie.

"And he's okay Signet, look! Now you can be together again. I'm so happy for you."

Finally realising how strange this conversation must appear to the animal carer, Signet clambered to her feet and offered a small, hopefully reassuring, smile. "Don't mind us, it's just a story we've been working on together," she said hastily. "An Australian faery tale, where swans turn into women, and ibises transform into wizards, or vice versa... It's for a school project."

She trailed off. Behind the khaki-clad woman, hovering in the entrance to one of the displays, Signet glimpsed a flash of a white-feathered cloak, and for a moment imagined there was a shadowy figure standing there watching her. An ibis who'd turned into a wizard.

She turned away. She didn't care about that now. She couldn't. Cobie was here, and she needed the zoo worker to leave them alone so she could try to talk with her beloved.

A loud bang, followed by the honk of an ibis and a kookaburra's gleeful cackle, sounded from a nearby enclosure, attracting the woman's attention. Shrugging her shoulders at Signet and Gracie, she hurried off to investigate.

Almost collapsing with relief, Signet spun around, and saw Gracie kneeling beside the water, hand reaching out to the swan. She froze, and watched the little girl curiously.

"Here beautiful Cobie, come and talk to us. Do you remember me? Daddy and I helped you that day in the park, and I've been wondering ever since if you were okay. We called so many people to try to find you, but you got lost in their system. I'm so glad you're all right. And I want to thank you, because it was your wife who helped me after I lost my mummy."

The swan had barely looked up when Gracie started talking, but now he was peering at her intently, head tilted slightly, seeming to be listening to her every word.

"You must have been so worried about your wife, and so desperate to return to her," she continued. "I know how much she missed you, and you must have missed her even more, because she is the kindest person I've ever known. Even though she was so sad, she gave up everything to help me and my daddy, because he lost his wife too."

Tears were streaking down Signet's face, and when Cobie finally looked up and saw her, she thought she might dissolve away to nothing. The joy was overwhelming, and her body tingled in recognition. She wondered if it was preparing to transform back to its true swan shape. She hoped so. More than anything she hoped so.

But a memory chilled her. When she'd changed from swan to human, Ibis Man had told her there was no going back. Had insisted that it was a one-way transformation, not something she could reverse, or do at will, like the seal sisters in the Selkie story. She hadn't cared then, because she'd been so focused on helping Gracie, and had resigned herself to the possibility that Cobie was lost to her.

But now? Here he was, and the darkest horror was rising within her. She shuddered, her stomach twisting as she tried to deny the heartbreaking situation she was in. There had to be a loophole, didn't there?

Sinking to the ground next to Gracie, she steeled herself, then gazed at her beloved.

"Hello my love," she began, before she trembled and her voice gave out. Tears gathered, and sobs racked her body.

Gracie put her small hand on Signet's shoulder, and smiled bravely. "We'll figure out what to do later, but for now, just tell Cobie that you're safe, and you still love him." She squeezed her shoulder. "I'm going to see the joey again, so you can be alone together."

Signet spent the afternoon with her beloved, speaking to him in a low voice, not caring when people came close and gave her funny looks. She told him how sorry she was about what had happened, how frantic she'd been when he didn't return, and how Gracie's pain had led her to try to help the young girl.

Eventually she lapsed into silence. She had no idea whether Cobie could understand what she was saying, but just being with him was calming her, and she hoped it was the same for him. Smiling, she reached out a hand to him, and was grateful when he bowed his head so she could pat him, then nestled in to her touch. "Oh my love," she said, sighing as tears rolled down her face once more.

When she heard footsteps approaching, she scrubbed at her eyes and tried to compose herself, then sagged with relief when it was Gracie who knelt down beside her.

"The zoo's closing for the day, so we have to leave," the little girl said, her voice cracking with regret. "But we can come back again as often as you like."

Drawing Gracie into her arms, Signet hugged her fiercely, then turned back to her beloved. "I'm so sorry dear Cobie, I have to go. But I'll be back, I promise. And I'll figure something out."

Tenderly she stroked his soft head one more time, then quickly stood up and walked away, without a backward glance. She knew she would dissolve into tears if she caught his eye again.

Chapter 18

It was a restless night of almost-sleep for Signet, her mood swinging from delight that she'd found Cobie, to aching despair that she was separated from him by a gulf even wider than not knowing where he was. Physical distance was one thing, but now she was trapped in human form while he remained a swan, and she didn't know if he could understand anything she said to him – or even recognised who she was. Fury and self-loathing pulsed through her, and tears that she hadn't waited for him poured from her eyes, chasing away the joy that she'd found him and knew he was safe.

In the brief respite when sleep dragged her under, dark shapes rose up from the zoo's pond and swallowed her beloved whole, and her anguished screams woke her back up.

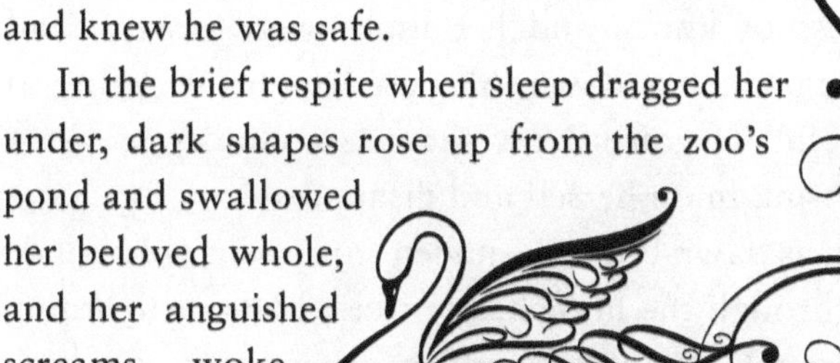

In the midnight dark she crept over to her wardrobe and tore her cloak of black swan feathers from its hanger. Draping it over her shoulders, she waited, breath held, an urgent prayer on her lips.

Could she change back?

Had the Ibis Man been wrong about that?

Was he just trying to scare her when he said she had to sacrifice her life as a swan in order to become human?

No. No. No.

Nothing happened. The feathers remained an external garment, scratching deep red welts into her skin as punishment, and she sank to the floor in a pool of sorrow and bitter tears. A single black feather floated to the carpet, and she picked it up and gripped it anxiously. Then she started laughing, on the verge of hysteria, when she contemplated how funny it would have been if it *had* worked, and she'd transformed back into a swan, locked in a city apartment. No hands to open the fridge for food, or unlock the door to get out. No voice to call for help.

But her laughter soon turned to tears again, and she cried until her throat burned and her chest ached.

Her whole body throbbed with pain, her stomach was a twisted mess of knots, and her limbs were heavy, dead weights dragging her down. She used to be so light, so elegant, so full of grace. Now she was a clumsy monster, trying to shrink in on herself and disappear.

Outside, as dawn broke, a sudden storm sent wild winds thrashing through the branches of trees, bolts of lightning flashing through the gloom, and a driving rain crashing against her building. For a moment she imagined walking outside and letting herself drown in its fury, or returning to the park and sinking to the bottom of her lake.

But she didn't even have the energy or the will to rise and close the window, remaining where she was, shivering on the wet carpet, the deluge drenching her and chilling her to the bone.

She drifted for a while, her mind a blur of recrimination and regret, until the high pitch of her alarm clock startled her back to wakefulness.

Gracie.

Dragging herself up off the floor and into the shower, she tried to get her emotions under control. To disguise the pale, trembling wreck she had become. This whirling ruin of fear and horror.

Slowly making her way up to Gracie's apartment, she clutched the feather that had fallen from her cloak in one hand, held like a talisman against her grief. Just before she knocked on the door she buried it in her bag though, her feelings too tender to have them recognised, to have to speak about this awful situation.

Somehow she managed to hold herself together, to greet Daniel and make Gracie's lunch, then head off to school with her young charge. The sun was shining, the birds were tweeting, and it was like nothing had happened yesterday. Like her heart hadn't been ripped out of her chest and torn into tiny pieces. Was it all just a dream?

When they reached the school gates, Gracie stopped suddenly. "Why are you so sad?" she asked.

For one glorious moment, Signet was filled with hope that she'd imagined it all. Gracie hadn't really spotted Cobie at the zoo, it had all been a feverish dream. And she hadn't actually recognised Signet as the mumma swan from the park, that conversation in front of the zoo worker was just another part of her bizarre nightmare.

None of it was real, surely.

Perhaps she hadn't even been to the zoo. Was she coming down with an illness or something? Fever was one of the first symptoms the girl in Gracie's class had suffered when she contracted measles a few weeks ago, although thankfully she was isolated before it could spread through the school.

Signet put her hand to her forehead. Was it warm? "I think I'm coming down with something," she replied. "I'll go home now and rest up. I'll be fine."

Gracie gazed up at her and smiled. "You are the mumma swan, aren't you?" she asked softly.

Shocked, Signet stared at her, eyes wide with fear. "No, that's impossible. That couldn't actually happen. It's just a faery tale, right?" It sounded even crazier coming from the mouth of a child than it had in her feverish brain.

Rolling her eyes, Gracie tugged on Signet's hand, until she squatted down to the little girl's eye level. "But we saw your husband yesterday," she insisted. "And I know he recognised you. He even remembered me."

Joy, longing, hope and fear collided within Signet, a constellation of stars exploding into a light that illuminated the universe – then disappeared into the darkness of the deepest black hole just as fast. "But how could you know that?" she whispered, voice scratchy and broken.

Shrugging, Gracie leaned over to wipe a tear from Signet's eye. "Your husband has a tiny white star just under his chin. And I don't know, something about the way he held his head, and dipped his beak to drink the water."

Signet laughed, bordering on hysteria again. "That's amazing. But how could you know what *I* am?"

"I didn't really, not until I saw you yesterday, talking with your husband. But then it all made sense. You listen to me the same way the mumma swan did, with your head tilted slightly – like you're doing right now! And you came to help me and Daddy after I complained to swan-you about Ingrid, the very day she quit."

Shaking her head in amazement, Signet managed a wan smile. "True, the depth of your pain that day is what made me transform. I wanted to help you, to look after you."

"Like you always did for your swan family, until your babies left home and your husband was taken away," Gracie said, patting Signet's hand like she had at the zoo, comforting her as though their roles were reversed, and she was the adult looking after the child.

"Also, the first time we went to the park together, you said you loved how I always made sure that everyone got some food – but how could you have known that, unless you'd been in the park with me before, as a swan?"

Signet laughed. "I thought you hadn't noticed that slip of the tongue. You are far smarter than me sweetie."

Giggling, Gracie shook her head. "That's not true – you're the one who changed from a swan into a person, like in the faery tale. And that was another clue. When you read me the story about the selkie woman whose sealskin was stolen by that nasty man to make her marry him, you seemed so puzzled that it could be taken away from her. And then I saw your cloak of swan feathers, and just knew it was your sealskin."

In the distance, they heard the school bell ring, and Gracie sighed. "I have to go in. But why do you look so sad still? Now you can be with your husband again. It's just like the story, but better. You've found your true love, and you already have your cloak, so you can change back. I'll be okay without you now, I promise."

Tears spilled over Signet's lashes, rivers of pain and anguish Gracie didn't understand, and couldn't stem. "What's wrong?" the little girl implored.

"I can't change back," Signet whispered, a shudder racking her body. "The Ibis Man said it only works once. That I can never go back to being a swan. Oh, I should never have become a human," she wailed. "Poor Cobie is trapped at the zoo without me."

Gracie patted her arm again. "But you shouldn't be sad, because if you never became a person, you still wouldn't know where your husband was. You'd be waiting all alone in the park, scared he was dead, with no one to comfort you, and no idea if you'd ever see him again. You had to become a human to discover where he was, and know that he's okay."

"Gracie!"

They both looked up guiltily as Janine shouted across the playground to where they still stood together, crouched at the gate.

"Come on, you're late! Hurry up!" the teacher shouted.

Signet forced the brightest smile she could. "Go on, you have a good day. I'll be here this afternoon when school gets out."

Her young charge threw her arms around her, hugging her tight, then smiled. "I'll see you then. And we'll figure it out. I'm so happy for you Mrs Swan!"

And she turned and ran to the entrance, and disappeared inside.

Chapter 19

As she watched Gracie enter the school building and be swallowed up, Signet stayed where she was, rooted to the spot with shock and pain. Shock that the young girl had discovered her secret and unravelled her heart, and the deepest anguish that she had found her beloved, yet was now even further away from him. When she hadn't known his fate, the secret hope of one day being reunited had swirled around her like the jacaranda blossoms Gracie loved so much, lending a lightness to her being, and sustaining her through the heavy darkness of fear.

Now that had all crumbled to dust, and she felt her heart breaking all over again.

But she couldn't stand here all day, staring at the school as she cried enough tears to drown herself. To drown the whole world.

Somehow Gracie still had faith it would all work out, and so, at least for today, she had to focus on that.

Impatiently scrubbing at her wet face, she forced a smile for the man who was looking at her with questioning eyes, and headed home. Her restless feet kept walking though, past her apartment block, across the road and into the park. Climbing the hill, her legs felt leaden, yet these human limbs were so much stronger now than they'd been that first day, when she'd staggered unsteadily out of the lake onto dry land, unfamiliar with her new body, and her new self.

At the summit, she lifted her arms and spun around, gazing with her human eyes at the sparkling city behind her, the bright sun above her, and the peaceful watery realm she'd inhabited for so long below her. It almost made her cry again, to picture Cobie gliding across the lake towards her, but the warmth on her shoulders filled her with a sense of possibility, purpose and potential, and Gracie's words echoed in her mind.

Yes, there must be a solution.

Lifting the hem of her long dress, she ran down the other side of the hill, skirting the water and heading for the trees. Breathing in the scent of the flowers and the earth, she felt a connection to the land as strong as her bond with the lake, and it gave her the strength to push on.

Cautiously she entered the woodland, her heart beating faster with anticipation and nerves. As a swan this part of the park had always seemed so dim and gloomy, but today, in her human guise, she loved the cool air and the lemony fragrance of the trees, the twittering of birds overhead, and the little creature burrows and hiding places for faeries. She strode onward, eyes peeled for Ibis Man.

Just as she was beginning to worry that she wouldn't find him, the shadows ahead of her rippled and danced, and he stepped out of the darkness into a column of sunbeams, his white-feathered cloak radiant in the sunlight.

"Signet," he said, bowing his head to her.

"Oh, thank goodness," she whispered, shoulders slumping with relief.

He took her hand and guided her to a fallen log, where they sat together in silence. There was so much she wanted to ask him, that she didn't know where to start. Then she wondered if he'd known Cobie was okay when he advised her that night, and if he had, why he didn't tell her.

Her mind raced, her chest tightened and her stomach fluttered, and she swayed, light-headed and fuzzy with confusion. Would she have transformed if she knew that her beloved was still alive?

Reaching out a calming hand to steady her, the wizened old man smiled. "You have done very good work Signet. The tantrum you witnessed from Gracie was not isolated. Her grief after losing her mother, and her hurt at feeling neglected by her father, was changing her as fundamentally as *you* changed, making her angry and impatient, and blocking off her beautiful heart. But you stopped it. Reversed it. You've helped your young charge immeasurably, and will continue to assist her as she grows up."

Pride and horror clashed within Signet. She was happy, and proud, that she'd been able to make things easier for Gracie and Daniel, who she'd come to love like her own family. But the pronouncement that she would still be assisting in the future made her heart sink. That sounded like she was trapped forever as a human. Fated to be eternally separated from her beloved.

"What's wrong?" he asked her softly.

Shrugging with despair, she turned to face him, her eyes imploring him to help her. "I found Cobie yesterday. He's alive."

"So why are you sad? That's wonderful news, isn't it?" he asked, voice wavering with confusion.

"Yes, of course, but he's a swan, and I'm... not. I'm trapped in the human world forever..." She trailed off, then looked up at him hopefully. "*Am* I trapped forever?"

A gentle breeze lifted the feathers in his cloak, reminding her of the ibises. He frowned. "I'm sorry Signet, but yes, you are. We talked about that when you were changing, that if you made the choice to become human, there was no going back. You can't transform again."

Signet's heart broke in two, then shattered into a million tiny shards. She lowered her head into her hands as tears started falling. Sobs shook her body, and she struggled to breathe. Ibis Man patted her back, trying to soothe her, but she couldn't be comforted. It felt like she was losing Cobie all over again.

A child's voice floated down the path towards them, followed by the ringing of a bike bell, and Signet looked up in alarm. Turning back to her companion, she was deflated to find herself alone. He'd faded back into the shadows, melting away into the darkness that suddenly surrounded Signet, drawing her under, and out.

She spent the day in a fog of delirium, sitting on the log for hours in a daze, then heading to the lake to try to speak to the swamp hens, to no avail. Finally she dozed off, one hand in the water, but her body on dry land. Partly connected to all the elements, but no longer wholly of one or the other.

When she woke up, the sun had shifted dramatically in the sky, and she choked down her rising panic. She had to pick Gracie up.

By the time she got to the school she'd at least partly composed herself, and she managed to keep her emotions under control while she and Gracie walked home, then spent the afternoon doing homework, cooking, and watching a little mindless television.

As she tucked Gracie in that night, the little girl looked up at her and smiled. "I'm so glad we found your husband."

Feigning happiness, Signet tried to swallow down her sadness and despair. "Me too."

"Shall we visit him on Saturday, or are you going to see him tomorrow?" Gracie yawned, and her eyes fluttered closed for a moment. "Or we could do both..."

Leaning down to kiss the little girl's forehead, Signet stifled her own yawn, worn out by the emotional pain and chaos of the last two days. "Thanks sweetie. We'll see what happens. You should go to sleep now."

"Mmm," Gracie murmured, as she drifted off.

Signet stayed at Gracie's window, staring out into the darkness and trying to fight off the black void circling her, until Daniel finally got home from work and she could go downstairs and cry herself to sleep.

Chapter 20

After dropping Gracie at school the following day, Signet caught the bus down to the quay, then the ferry across the harbour to the zoo. Mist wreathed the shoreline, and as she stepped into its cool embrace, she wished it could transport her to another realm, one where she was a swan again, and her beloved had never been hurt, never been taken so far away from her. A place where they were gliding across their sun-dazzled lake together, wings touching, hearts entwined.

She missed him so much, with a yearning that was splitting her soul in two.

But as she stumbled on a crack in the pavement on her way up the hill, her breath caught. What if it wasn't the same for Cobie? Did a swan feel emotions as profoundly as a human did? Was his grief and longing as acute as hers – as deep as the harbour, as a bottomless well? Or was he content with his new life in the wetland area of the zoo? Had he made new friends, even found a new partner to replace her?

Her blood ran cold, and she sank to the ground in horror. Her whole body shook with fear. She didn't have the strength to face this possibility, couldn't risk him staring blankly at her, or swimming away.

A hand emerged from the mists and grabbed her shoulder, and she screamed.

"I'm sorry Miss, I didn't mean to scare you." The man dressed in the khaki uniform of the zoo was apologetic, almost sheepish. "Are you okay? Do you need help?"

Signet forced a polite smile, though her cheeks burned with embarrassment. "Thank you, but I'm all right."

She allowed him to help her to her feet, then she turned and fled back down the hill, and onto a ferry home.

That night she tossed and turned, filled with dread and self-recrimination. Unable to sleep a wink. Tortured by a starless black void where she floated forever alone. When she dragged herself upstairs the next morning, she was bleary eyed and grumpy, but Gracie wasn't offended, prattling on about her upcoming sports day, and finally winning a half smile from Signet when she admitted how disastrously her show and tell had gone the day before.

At the school gate, Gracie hugged Signet fiercely, and told her to be brave, then raced off across the playground.

She was right, Signet mused. She couldn't be a coward, and she couldn't wait any longer. If Cobie had forgotten her, she needed to know. And if he hadn't, she should be there to make sure he didn't have the chance.

This time she stepped confidently off the ferry and hurried up the hill, then showed her ticket and entered the zoo before she could second-guess herself. Nervously she approached the wetland lake where she'd found Cobie, and her heart lightened and her mood shifted when he swam right over to her, and bent towards her so she could stroke his soft black head.

Tears welled, but Signet gulped them back down, refusing to let them fall. She would be brave.

"Hello my sweet," she whispered, and smiled when he gazed up at her, head tilted as he listened.

"I'm sorry I couldn't come yesterday. I tried to. I almost made it through the entrance, but then I got scared and ran away, like a coward. I'm just so worried that you've forgotten me, or even worse, that you haven't missed me."

Her voice hitched. It was strange, this one-sided conversation, but she took a deep breath and continued. "I wouldn't blame you I guess. I mean, it's been several months since you were injured, and the wildlife worker brought you here to be healed…"

It was scary, how long they'd been apart. Could she expect him to remember her? Helplessly she gazed at him, torn, and almost ready to flee again. But he came up out of the water and crept a little closer, settling down next to Signet and laying his head in her lap. Some of the knots of tension in her shoulders released, and she sighed with relief.

"Excuse me," someone said behind her, and she slowly turned, a hand still on Cobie's body. Touching him was comforting her, and hopefully it was helping him too.

"Yes?" she asked anxiously.

"Well, ah, no one is supposed to touch the animals, but this one clearly trusts you. Would you like to feed him?

He's been fretting all this week, and refusing to eat. Maybe he'll accept it from you?"

"I'd love to," she murmured, and tried hard not to beam with relief and joy. She didn't want Cobie to not eat, didn't want him to get sick, but as awful as it sounded, she hoped this meant he did remember her. That her visit on Sunday had stirred something within him, and he had been as distraught as she was the last few days at being apart.

"Oh, can I ask you something?"

The zoo keeper nodded.

"I heard that this swan had been injured. Is he okay now? Can he still fly?"

He gazed at her curiously. "He was injured, yes, a few months ago now. But he recovered quite well, and quite quickly, in our animal hospital. But we clip the flying feathers of our birds here, so they don't fly away and become lost, and either starve to death or get hit by a car."

"Thank you," she whispered, then turned back to Cobie. She'd been wondering if he had tried to fly home to their park once he was well, but maybe it was a good thing he hadn't been able to, because it was a very long way for a bird to fly.

Cheered a little, she offered Cobie the lettuce, spinach, corn and peas, and he nibbled them from her open palm, careful not to hurt her, while the zoo worker fed the remaining animals, then left them alone.

The day passed in a flash, and Signet was shocked when someone called out the time to a friend. She had to get back to Gracie!

Gently patting her beloved one more time, she bid him farewell and promised to return the next morning. And she did, spending all of her time between dropping Gracie off and picking her up from school at the zoo with Cobie. Sometimes she talked to him, other times they just sat quietly together, his head in her lap, Signet dreaming of her past as a swan, and drowning in regret. And every afternoon, when she had to leave, her heart broke all over again.

Her pulse quickening in anticipation, Signet waited at the zoo entrance before it opened on Saturday morning, bouncing up and down in her eagerness to get in and see Cobie. Daniel and Gracie had gone to visit her grandmother for the weekend, so she was free to spend two whole uninterrupted days with her beloved.

There were a lot more people there than usual though, a lot more noise, and a lot more children eager to feed the birds and try to pat the swans. Cobie was visibly distressed by all the attention, so Signet reluctantly told him to swim out to the small island in the centre to have a break. "I'm not leaving though," she whispered. "I'll come back when the crowds thin out."

He nodded, or so she desperately wanted to believe, then swam across the lake out of the reach of the children and their grabby hands. Standing up to head to the cafe, she was startled when a huge white ibis flew down and landed next to her. She stared at him, eyebrows raised, wondering if it was the feather-cloaked old man who'd helped her, in his creature guise. Could *he* change back and forth from human to bird? Was there a way to master the transformation? Or was Ibis Man as trapped as she was in his human form, and feeling just as bereft as her?

Shaking her head to dislodge the wild hope that had sprung up, she brushed past the bird. She needed something to eat. Something to ground her back in the reality of her fractured life, and stop the wishful thinking that was making her head spin.

In the afternoon, as the sun started to sink in the west and the whole world was soaked in golden light, Signet returned to the wetlands area, and was overjoyed when Cobie paddled across the dazzling lake towards her. Relieved the crowds here had thinned out as everyone jostled for position at the final seal show of the day, she smiled in gratitude as her beloved hauled himself out of the water and came to sit beside her on the lake's edge, one wing extended so they were almost holding hands.

Time slowed, the noise dimmed, and a strange mist descended over them. Signet felt a touch of enchantment swirling around them, cutting them off from the real world, and she imagined she could hear Cobie talking to her, telling her how much he'd missed her, and how often he had prayed she would somehow find him. She told him about her life too, and when a cool breeze made her shiver, he reached his wing further around her, sheltering her from the cold. Just as he always had.

Hearing the honk of an ibis, she glanced at her watch, and gasped. It was long past closing time. Slowly she became aware of the absence of human chatter, of the lights going out, and of the swell of animal calls around her. Somehow the mist had hidden her from view, and now she was locked in the zoo. She laughed with joy. She and Cobie had the whole night together.

But when she gazed down at him, the pain of her loss returned, despair making her body ache.

"Oh Cobie, what are we going to do? I don't want to cause you any distress by being here, if you even know that it's me. Maybe I should let you find a new partner, someone to comfort you the way only a swan can…" She broke off as he stood up and flapped his wings, seeming agitated.

Did he understand what she was saying?

"I'm so desperately sorry that I didn't wait for you, that I didn't trust. If only I'd known, I wouldn't have changed, I promise you. Although Gracie pointed out that I wouldn't know you were okay if I was still a swan, so…"

She trailed off, the sadness that was pulsing through her so thick she could taste it. Could hold it in her hands, and in her heart. A physical weight that could drown her.

Tears welled, hot and thick, and this time she couldn't hold them back. "I can't be brave like you Cobie, it hurts too much. I can't contemplate a life without you."

Cobie was staring at her, following the track of her tears down her cheek, watching as they hit the surface of the lake and rippled outward across the water, which was now illuminated by the golden light of the rising full moon.

Signet sobbed, eyes closed, heart broken, hands clutching at her beloved. When he squawked, she prised her heavy lids open, vision blurry, and saw him dip his long neck to the dark water. Watched in wonder as he drank one of her glittering tears, then reached out his wing to her in comfort.

Through gritty lids she stared at him, daring to hope for just a moment that the magic that transformed her into a woman could work for her beloved too. But as the moon sailed across the sky and the midnight hour came and went, nothing happened. Her heart turned to ice, and she shook with despair. Closing her eyes to block out the physical reminder of her pain, she surrendered to the sinking sensation in her body and drifted off, curled up in the shelter of Cobie's wing, head on his warm, solid, feathered body.

Loved, but more lost than she had ever been.

Chapter 21

A stern peck on her foot and the honk of a swamp hen woke Signet. Opening her eyes, she blinked in confusion. Above her stretched a pale shimmery arc of blue sky, instead of the grey of her bedroom ceiling, and the grass was cold and slightly scratchy beneath her, a million miles from her cosy bed. Was she a swan again?

Squinting in the pre-dawn light, she tried to figure out where she was, and why. Slowly things started coming back to her. She'd spent yesterday with Cobie at the zoo, and must have fallen asleep by his side. Yet now her head was supported on a strong, muscled thigh, and there was a man's arm around her waist.

What?

Alarmed, she tried to focus, and saw a dark-haired stranger smiling down at her.

Sitting up in shock, she pulled away from him and shuffled backwards, panicked. She glanced wildly around the wetland area. Where was Cobie? And who on earth was *he*?

She peeked at him again, taking in the dancing eyes and the long, thick black hair. His smile disarmed her, and there was a familiar twinkle in his gaze.

Cobie?

"Is it really you?" she whispered.

Slowly the man nodded, but there was something tentative and unsure in his expression. And then his features twisted in pain.

He was still changing. Signet tried to recall how she'd felt as she transformed from swan to human. The strange elongation of limbs, the tearing pain, the heaviness of her bones, the terror at what was happening. Gently she took his hand, trying to reassure him. And realised that he was naked under his black-feathered cloak.

Blushing, she glanced away, and saw a blur of white out of the corner of her eye. Ibis Man approached, a pair of khaki pants and a shirt like the zoo workers wore over one arm. Wordlessly he handed them to Cobie, winked at Signet, then withdrew, fading back into the shadows as the beautiful colours of dawn made way for the morning.

When she turned back to Cobie, shivering with cold, he was dressed. He placed his cloak around her shoulders, then drew her into the warmest embrace she'd ever experienced. Human hugs were a form of deep magic. Closing her eyes, she melted into him, and felt all the pain and stress and fear fall away.

"I've missed you so much," he said, voice raspy, and filled with longing. "I was so scared when I woke up in the hospital here, being poked and prodded, my wing immobilised. Then after I recovered I kept waiting to be taken home to you, but it never happened. And as each day passed, my hope faded, and I was starting to wonder how I could go on."

Signet's heart broke at his words, then was stitched back together again by the feel of his arms around her. "My love, I was so miserable too, and completely lost without you. Then finding you last week was amazing, until I realised that I couldn't change back into a swan. But now..."

She stared up at him, took his face in her hands, and gently kissed him. It really was as amazing as those romance novels made out. Behind them, a kookaburra laughed, and Signet whipped around. Workers were starting to visit the enclosures, pushing trolleys of feed, opening and closing doors, and setting up for the day.

"We should get out of here," she said urgently. "Before we have to explain our presence."

Hand in hand, they ducked out of the entrance and headed down to the ferry, and Signet laughed in delight as she watched Cobie lost in the beauty of the harbour and the glittering city. She couldn't wait to show him her new world. *Their* new world.

When they reached her apartment, she unlocked the door, then nervously welcomed him in. He gazed around himself, bewildered, and she remembered how confusing her first days in the human world had been. She would take it slow for him, and share the guidebook she'd been given, but she hoped that having her at his side would make it easier for him.

After hanging his feather cloak up next to hers in the bedroom, and grinning as she discovered some men's jeans and shirts had been added to the wardrobe, she made a pot of herbal tea and arranged a platter of fruit salad for their breakfast. They talked for hours, of how she'd found her way in this crazy new existence, what it was like spending time with Gracie, and how she'd made friends with the little girl's teacher Janine, and learned about yoga, dancing and romance novels.

At times they lapsed into silence, too overcome for words, just staring into each other's eyes, holding hands, and smiling with relief that they'd found each other again. Signet couldn't wrap her head around how the magic had happened, or what immense power there was in a tear, but she was grateful for it.

Later, after they'd had lunch and flicked through the *How To Be Human* guidebook, Cobie suddenly looked anxious, then gazed at her shyly. "And, um, Gracie's dad?" he asked, a hint of fear in his voice, and... *jealousy?*

Signet smiled. "I think Gracie has her heart set on him being with Janine one day, which Janine would love too. But there's no rush, and he still has some healing to do before he'd be ready for that..."

Sighing with relief, Cobie leaned over and kissed his beloved. "I'm so glad you waited for me, that you didn't replace me. And that you found me." He speared another grape with his fork, and popped it in his mouth. "I'm even more glad that I'm here now, in this form. Seeing you every day at the zoo, but not being able to tell you how I felt, that I knew you, and I loved you, was torture."

"For me too," Signet said. "I didn't know if you could understand me, or even recognised me. And I was scared that I was causing you more pain with my presence."

"Never. And I never want to be parted from you again."

A smile lit up Signet's face. "Me either. And we won't, I promise. Human or swan, you're my forever love."

That afternoon, when Cobie had grown into his body and felt more comfortable in his new skin, they left the safety of the apartment and crossed the road to their park, and sat on the grass together gazing out over the lake. Signet told him about their last swan babies, Penny and Seth, and how they'd both eventually found the confidence to fly off and start their grown-up lives. Laughing, she recalled the grumpy swamp hen who'd woken her up just in time to pick Gracie up on her first day, then she spoke again of her devotion to the lonely little girl.

"You'll love her too," she said, heart lifting with joy and contentment. "And she already adores you. It was she who spotted you first, at the zoo, and she's the one who gave me the strength to keep coming back."

Cobie smiled. "I can't wait to meet her, so I can thank her, but to be honest I'd be happy if I never met a single human, and we got to spend all our days alone together."

"Me too." Signet leaned into him, comforted by his presence, and feeling more truly herself than she ever had.

Maybe that is the real magic – discovering who you are meant to be, who you truly are, and feeling secure enough within yourself to be it. And perhaps real love is finding the person who honours that and reflects it back to you. The one who sees you, the real you, and who brings out the very best in you, encouraging you to be all that you can be, all you dream of being.

As the sun prepared to set, they climbed the hill and sat together, arms wrapped around each other, marvelling as the sky turned every shade of pink-orange-lavender, and their lake transformed to liquid gold. Slowly twilight descended, and they watched two swans fly in from the south, their wings touching, before they swooped down and landed on the log that jutted out into the water, the log they'd so often sat on together.

Cobie grinned at his swan maiden wife. "It's Penny!"

Together he and Signet ran down the hill, their tears mixing with laughter and streaming out behind them, soft whispers on the wind that told a story of love, family and togetherness despite all the obstacles they'd faced. They stood on the shore hand in hand, smiling as their daughter swam towards them with her partner in tow.

Signet crouched down, and slowly, gently, extended her hand, overcome with emotion when Penny angled her head up to be patted.

"Oh darling girl, I'm so glad you've come back home. This can be your realm now, since we have a new home in that building over there. And we'll come and see you often, and bring you some treats."

She gazed up at Cobie, eyes sparkling with joy. "Who knows, maybe we'll be grandparents one day."

From the woodland, a kookaburra laughed, then the lights in the park came on. A cool breeze made Cobie shiver, and Signet rubbed her hands over his arms, trying to warm him. "We should get home, make some dinner. Bye darling Penny, we'll see you soon."

Signet's heart was full as they made their way back to the road, Cobie still anxious as a fast car sped through the red traffic light. She remembered how terrified she'd been that first night. "Don't worry, you'll get used to it, I promise," she said, kissing him on the cheek as they waited for the light to change. She still couldn't believe that she'd found him, and he'd been able to transform too. Now they had their whole human lives ahead of them, years stretching out to discover the world, and each other.

As they turned in to their apartment complex, Gracie and her dad were getting out of a cab, and the little girl squealed when she saw them, and ran full tilt at them. She hugged Signet tight, then threw her arms around Cobie.

"Oh, I'm so happy to finally meet you! Daddy, this is Signet's husband, Cobie!"

Daniel extended his hand, and grasped Cobie's. "It's a pleasure to meet you. I can't tell you how grateful we both are to your wife, for her wonderful caring of us."

"And I'm grateful to you both for looking after my wife while I was away," he said with a smile.

Biting her lip nervously, Signet looked at Daniel. "Well, um, technically we're not actually married yet, because Cobie had to go away before we could, but..."

Gracie's eyes lit up. "Ooh, we can organise your wedding! That will be brilliant! I can be your flower girl, and Daddy can be the best man, and Miss Henwood can be your maid of honour. Please Signet, can we do it? Pretty please! Can we make your happily ever after happen?"

Taking Cobie's hand in hers, Signet smiled at the father-and-daughter family she'd grown to feel part of.

"Yes. That would be a dream come true."

"Hope is the thing with feathers,
That perches in your soul,
And sings the tune without the words."
Emily Dickinson, American poet

"In a utilitarian age, of all other times,
it is a matter of grave importance that
faery tales should be respected."
Charles Dickens, English writer

Thank You!

Thank you so much for reading this book, and sharing the magic of Signet and Gracie's stories. As an indie author, I rely on word of mouth and reader reviews to get the word out. If you enjoyed *The Swan Maiden*, I would be so grateful if you could take a moment to leave a review on any book site, or tag me on facebook or instagram if you post about it. Reviews can help improve sales and ranking, and are of immense help to all indie writers. Even a single sentence will make a difference, and might help a new reader decide to give it a try.

If you'd like to stay in touch and receive free exclusive content, be the first to hear about book news, events info and giveaways, win prizes and more, you can sign up for my newsletter at

www.sereneconneeley.com/subscribe.

(And don't worry, you can unsubscribe at any time...)

With love and gratitude,
Serene xx

Black Swans

The black swan (cygnus atratus) is a large, long-necked water bird native to Australia, which lives in estuaries, waterways, lakes and wetlands. They appear to be all black, but have white primary wing feathers that become visible when they fly, and swoop across the water.

They aren't migratory animals, but they may travel to find better water or food supplies when necessary. If they successfully breed somewhere, they are likely to stay. My backyard park has two adult swans who have been there for years, and have successfully reared several clutches of babies. And in the Gippsland area of Victoria, many swan couples have made their permanent home there on the lakes, peacefully co-existing with boats, traffic and people.

Black swans are the state emblem of Western Australia, and are protected under the Australian National Parks and Wildlife Act of 1974. They've been introduced to other countries, including New Zealand, Sweden and the UK. The first black swan was taken to England in 1791 – they became popular for private collections and zoos, but some escaped, so there are now many that live in the wild.

Black swans pair for life and share parenting duties, which is why they've come to symbolise romance, equality, and the joy of helping others, as well as inner mysteries and creative expression. Both parents alternate time on the nest, and both raise their children. The mother swan usually lays an egg a day, for a clutch of eggs between one and nine. Black swans often have two clutches a year.

The eggs incubate for six to seven weeks before the babies hatch. Cygnets are pale grey when born, with fuzzy down instead of feathers, and black beaks instead of red. They can swim and feed themselves as soon as they're born, but can't fly. They grow and change rapidly – it's a beautiful, fascinating thing to watch them grow up day by day.

Their parents teach them to fly when they are between five and seven months old, which is extraordinary to witness (I've posted a few videos on my instagram account @sereneconneeley). At some point after that they will leave their parents to find their own territory and partner.

An adult female swan is called a pen, hence Penny and Pennington; an adult male is a cob, from the Middle English word cobbe ("leader of a group"), hence Cobie and Jacob; and a baby is a cygnet, from the Latin cygnus ("swan") and the Old French suffix -et ("little"), hence Signet and Siggy.

Black swans are mostly vegetarian, grazing all day on algae and submerged weeds, which they reach by plunging their long necks into the water. Occasionally they'll graze on land, eating grasses and clover, but they're quite clumsy – a strange contrast to their elegance on the water. Black swans are gentle by nature, but they are territorial, and will fiercely protect their cygnets if they feel threatened. They have no teeth, but can still latch on if attacked. (It feels a bit tickly when they eat clover leaves from your hand ☺)

There are seven species of swans. The others are the European mute and whooper swans, the North American trumpeter and tundra swans, the Eurasian bewick swans, and the South American black-necked swans.

Swans are intelligent, and remember people who treat them well. Although the ones in our park are very defensive when most dogs approach, hissing and puffing up to appear bigger (a natural reaction because a dog killed a swan a few years ago), there are a few dogs they are fine with, and they'll sit calmly with them and just watch each other, because they know they are not a threat.

"Goodbyes are only for those who love with their eyes.
Because for those who love with heart and soul,
There is no such thing as separation."
Rumi, Persian poet

With Thanks

I am so grateful, as always, to my sweet hubby and precious beloved, for his love, support, and belief in me, and for the magical life we've created together in our cute little apartment on the edge of the city, next to our black-swan-visited park. Thank you for being my forever love.

Love and gratitude to my writer besties Selina A. Fenech and K. A. Last, for encouragement, critiques, sprints and retreats, cover assistance, and support, focus and action.

Many thanks to lovely voice actor Angela Peters for bringing Gracie and Signet so beautifully to life on the audiobook.

Much love to Jo Henwood, Ring Maiden of the Australian Fairy Tale Society (australianfairytalesociety.org), for faery-tale fun, friendship and inspiration, and to our wonderful Sydney group. It's always a joy to drink tea, share stories, plan events, and discuss life, love, politics and faery tales with you.

So much gratitude to Merrill, Katrina and Harold for your incredible care of our beautiful Sydney Park swan friends, and to George and Paynesville Swans for sharing the daily lives and adventures of your region's sweet creatures.

And all the love to my wonderful friends and family, especially Mum, Dad, Margie and Pete, who have loved and supported me always, encouraged my writing and love of reading, and given me the freedom to be my true self. And to Petie, my Other Dad, for a lifetime of love and laughter, music, mayhem and sport, political debate, spiritual discussions, and campaigning together for a better world. We all miss you so much ♥

With much love, Serene xx

With Love and Respect

I acknowledge the Gadigal People of the Eora Nation as the Traditional Custodians of the land on which I – and Signet and Cobie – live. I recognise their continuing connection to land, waters and culture, and pay my respects to their Elders past, present and emerging.

And I acknowledge the Traditional Owners of Country throughout Australia. Like many nations, we have a brutal history of invasion and colonisation, and I desperately hope that our government will finally start reflecting the will of the people for change, and take action now towards recognition and reconciliation.

#voicetreatytruth
fromtheheart.com.au

About the Author

Serene Conneeley is an Australian writer with a fascination for history, travel, ritual, and the myth and magic of ancient places and cultures. As well as her seven non-fiction titles and seven novels, she's written for magazines about news, travel, health, spirituality, entertainment, and social and environmental issues, was editor of several preschool magazines, and has contributed to books on witchcraft, history, psychic development and personal transformation.

She is a member of the Australian Fairy Tale Society, and has studied magical and medicinal herbalism, bereavement counselling, reconnective healing, reiki and many other healing modalities, plus politics and journalism.

Serene loves reading books, drinking tea, working out, visiting the swans in her backyard park, and celebrating the energy of the moon and the magic of the earth. Her pagan heart blossomed as she climbed mountains, sat in stone circles, crawled into ancient burial mounds and stood in the shadow of the pyramids on her travels, and she's also, perhaps more importantly, learned the magic of finding true happiness and peace at home.

www.SereneConneeley.com

Other Books by Serene

The Into the Mists Trilogy

Into the Mists

Into the Dark

Into the Light

Into the Mists: A Journal

The Into the Mists Trilogy Hardcover Omnibus

"I'm absolutely blown away by this series. It is beautiful from start to finish – magical, realistic, gentle, harsh, sad, joyful… I've been on a total rollercoaster ride, and now feel totally bereft at the thought that these wonderful people will no longer be part of my life. These books are just beautiful."
Kylie Matthews, reviewer

The Into the Storm Trilogy

Into the Storm

Into the Fire

Into the Air

The Into the Storm Trilogy Hardcover Omnibus

"This series is a transformative must-read. Profound, thought provoking and empowering, it's so immersive that the magic emanates from the pages. I loved every second of it."
Kastie Pavlik, author of the Children of the Morning Star Trilogy

The Magic Series (with Lucy Cavendish)

The Book of Faery Magic

Mermaid Magic: Connecting With the Energy
of the Ocean and the Healing Power of Water

Witchy Magic

"*Mermaid Magic* is a wonderfully inspiring read. It really made me want to shed my twenty-first century shackles and dive into the ocean to embrace its wonderful healing powers. Thank you magical ladies for the journey!"

Sabina Collins, reviewer

The Sacred Series

Seven Sacred Sites: Magical Journeys That Will
Change Your Life

A Magical Journey: Your Diary of Inspiration,
Adventure and Transformation

Sacred Journey: A Meditation To Connect
You To the Magic of the Earth

"*Seven Sacred Sites* is by far the best travel book this year. Serene's style evokes the great travel writers like James A Michener, who weave cultural anthropology into an entertaining traveller's tale. It's a recipe for pure reading pleasure."

Joanne Lock, Spheres magazine